For seven days, Lucinda had been locked in a room by Yankee soldiers.

When Lucinda heard a faint commotion shortly before noon, her first thought was that another prisoner was being brought in. But something was strange and frightening about the sounds she heard. Someone pounded up the stairs with heavy tread and ran down the hall.

Lucinda heard a key grating in the lock of a room across the hall...then steps moved toward her door and a key was fitted into its lock. She looked around the room for a hiding place, but there was none, nor was there anything she could use in self-defense. All Lucinda could do was move away from the door so she would be behind it when it opened.

The door flung open, and Lucinda's eyes widened in surprise as a blond soldier in federal blue entered the room, holding a pistol in his right hand. He whirled around and their eyes met.

"Hurry! We've got to get out of here."

Lucinda's vision blurred for a moment, then cleared as he came closer. "Ben!" she cried. "Wha—"

But he gave her no time to finish her questions as he half-led, half-pushed her from the room, down the stairs, past the crumpled figure of the guard, and out into the peaceful sunshine of a summer noon. Ben untied a horse from the hitching post and boosted Lucinda up behind him, and she scarcely had time to adjust her skirts before Ben had urged the horse to a canter.

"This is insane," Lucinda managed to say as they rounded a corner and started north on Madison Street.

"So are the Yankees," Ben replied without turning his head. "Just be quiet and trust me."

KAY CORNELIUS lives in Huntsville, Alabama, the setting for *More than Conquerors*. Her strong knowledge of history is apparent in this, her *Heartsong Presents* debut.

More than Conquerors

Kay Cornelius

Heartsong Presents

With love to Don, Kathy, Kevin, Amy, Ben,
Jake, and Kyle.

Thanks to Renée Pruitt of the Huntsville
Public Library Heritage Room, for her
assistance.

ISBN 1-55748-452-X

MORE THAN CONQUERORS

PRINTED IN THE U.S.A.

one

Lucinda Matthews stood on her tiptoes, trying to see over the heads of the people who lined the street around the Huntsville depot on this fair October day in 1861. The early autumn wind tugged at her bonnet, and impatiently she clapped a hand to the top of her head. An impromptu brass band made up of townspeople with varying degrees of talent played a military march with more spirit than skill and were wildly cheered when they ended their piece.

All eyes turned to the Memphis and Charleston Railroad Roundhouse, where the gray-clad troops of the Huntsville Rifles had formed up and now marched to the depot.

Lucinda leaned forward, her eyes eagerly scanning the ranks. Sunlight fired the officers' sabers and glinted on the brass buttons of the company's new gray uniforms. She had no trouble picking out the young lieutenant she had come to bid farewell, the tallest man in the company, but he was still too far away to see her in the crowd.

A makeshift speaker's platform had been erected on the south side of the depot, and a few local dignitaries sat near it, waiting for the company to halt. The crowd cheered that command as if the group executing it had already performed valorous deeds in the service of the Confederacy. They continued to cheer until Mayor Coltart stood.

Lucinda had heard the man's words before, when her brother Henry had left several months ago to join the Fourth Alabama in Virginia. While the mayor spoke of honor and duty and love of one's homeland, Lucinda kept her eyes on Ben Bradley. He stood with the others in the prescribed parade rest posture, his blue eyes staring straight ahead at a point somewhere above the speaker's head. His blond hair was almost totally hidden by the large hat, complete with feather, that he'd bought after he'd been elected to be one of the two lieutenants in the company.

Had he seen her? Lucinda looked down at her blue-sprigged muslin dress and wished she had something newer, something he had never seen her in, to wear at this last farewell. Once Ben had told her that he liked the dress because its flowers matched her eyes. She had laughed and invited him to look at her eyes, which weren't really blue at all, but a flinty gray.

The mayor finally concluded his flowery and elegant tribute and the band struck up a somewhat ragged rendition of "In Dixie's Land." Someone in front of her moved to speak to someone behind her, and Lucinda pushed forward, her eyes willing Ben Bradley to look her way.

"Ben! Over here!"

Ben Bradley smiled widely, his blue eyes sparkling with excitement, and came over to where she stood, taking both her hands in his.

"I feared you'd be gone before I got here," Lucinda said, suddenly shy.

"You know I wouldn't let the train leave until I told you goodbye," Ben said, never taking his gaze from her face.

"I brought you a ribbon." Lucinda took her right hand from his to reach into her pocket for the multi-colored band that all the girls were giving their special beaux to remember them by.

"I'll pin it on my collar," Ben said, taking it from her.

"I'm sure it'll bring me back safely."

"Oh, Ben, I hope so!" Lucinda exclaimed. "I. . .I'll be praying for that."

Ben's smile softened, and he looked at Lucinda so intently that she was sure he was going to kiss her right there, in front of the whole town. He took her hands in his again and squeezed them.

"Don't worry. Our rifles can show those Yankees a thing or two."

"It's no wonder, the way you've always hunted. But then, the 'coons and deer never shot back."

Although Lucinda was quite serious, Ben threw his head back and laughed, showing even, white teeth. Several people turned to watch them, so Ben drew Lucinda behind a stack of equipment the Huntsville Rifles were taking with them to Montgomery.

"Ah, Miss Lucinda, I'll miss you. I wish I could ask you to wait for me—"

"Hush, Ben!" Lucinda warned, not wanting to hear the words he'd tried to say several times since he'd known they were about to leave.

To her chagrin, Lucinda felt uncharacteristic tears coming to her eyes. She blinked fiercely in an attempt to defeat them, but succeeded only in sending two perfect teardrops down her cheeks.

"Oh, Miss Lucinda!" Ben groaned. He pulled her to him and bent his tall frame over to kiss her.

I'm going to faint, Lucinda thought, but of course she didn't. The only thing that would be worse than letting a young man kiss her in public would be to faint and call further attention to herself. Lucinda closed her eyes, painfully aware of the brass buttons on Ben's jacket, feeling that at any moment she would surely suffocate. Then Ben pulled away, and Lucinda saw that his eyes gleamed with unshed tears.

"Your family. . .," Lucinda began uncertainly, and he shook his head.

"They wouldn't come to the depot—said they don't like all the crowds and the fuss. But I'm awfully glad you came, and before much longer, you'll be seeing us coming back. Just you remember that."

"Yes." She wanted to add some profound words that he'd always remember. But a warning blast sounded from the locomotive, and the Huntsville Rifles began to board the waiting train. Bestowing a final light kiss on Lucinda's cheek, Ben left to join the others.

Lucinda watched Ben walk away, handsome in his new uniform, the saber his father had presented to him at his side. She felt a quiet exultation that this golden young man had singled her out for attention. Her cheeks were bright with becoming color as she called a last goodbye, aware that she was posing for a picture Ben would take to war with him. He turned and waved from the train. Too soon, the massive locomotive moved away, bearing its precious cargo to unknown perils.

Keep him safe, dear Lord, Lucinda prayed silently.

"Mercy, Miss Lucinda," a familiar voice said behind her. "What will people think, you a-throwin' yourself at Mr. Ben like that?"

"Oh, don't be cross, Viola. You shouldn't spy on me, you know," she added, smiling at the woman who had reared her since her mother's untimely death ten years ago, when Lucinda was only eight. Viola had come to the depot with her, stopping on the fringes of the crowd, where

Lucinda had hoped she would stay.

"Cross ain't the word," Viola muttered. "The very idea, lettin' a man get so clost to you in broad daylight, and you not spoken for!" She continued to mutter and fume as they turned south toward the center of town, walking to the Matthews' house on Adams Street.

"Mr. Ben is hardly a stranger, you know," Lucinda reminded her, but Viola merely shook her turbanned head and glared. Lucinda wondered who else had seen her kiss Ben. At least no one should be surprised, since the two of them had paired off for some months.

Vividly, Lucinda remembered the first time she'd noticed Ben Bradley as someone interesting, not just one of her older brother Henry's many friends. Last Christmas at Alice Ann's house, he had come into the hallway, loudly calling, "Christmas gift!" She had put her hair up that night for the first time and was wearing a green taffeta ball gown that had made her father gasp when he saw her in it. "You look so grownup—and so much like your mother," he had said.

Ben noticed Lucinda too. He asked her to dance and waltzed her to the mistletoe, kissing her cheek and laughing when she blushed. A few months later when the war started, Ben had joined the Huntsville Rifles. As the unit outfitted themselves and drilled for Confederate service, Ben had visited her often, always under the watchful eyes of Viola or her father. He had escorted her to the balls and farewell parties that filled the summer, flattering her with his attentions.

Life is strange, Lucinda thought. If the war hadn't interfered with Ben's plans to go to New Orleans to learn the cotton exporting business, Lucinda would never have gotten to know him better. It was presumed that he would pursue that occupation after the war ended—which everyone agreed couldn't be much longer.

Lucinda half-smiled, thinking of how both Ben and her brother Henry had feared that the war would be over before they could get into it. Well, Henry had already been involved in heavy fighting, and now Ben would have his chance. She felt her heart swell with pride for the bravery of all the young men in Confederate gray.

A chill autumn breeze stirred up a sudden swirl of leaves, and Lucinda's smile faded. With Ben and Henry and all the other young men gone, she faced a long and lonely winter.

Seth Russell, recently commissioned officer of the Fourth Ohio Cavalry, United States Army, was having trouble falling asleep the last night before reporting for duty.

He had no doubt that he was doing the right thing. He realized that the country his grandfather had been willing to die to bring into being was about to be destroyed, and he knew he must do all he could to help preserve the Union. Yet, noble as those motives might be, Seth had to acknowledge that his sense of restlessness had another cause.

Seth threw back the covers and walked to the window. Pulling aside the draperies, he opened the sash to admit the cool night air. With a practiced eye he scanned the heavens, locating the fall constellations. The Pleiades and Aldebaran were clustered together to the right of Capella, in the center, opposite Polaris. Already Orion, the hunter, had climbed above the horizon.

The stars and planets represented a constant in Seth's life. As a boy he had learned to find north by the Big Dipper and had read stories about Cassiopeia and Hercules and Orion, Gemini and Jason. Later, as a student in Ormsby Mitchel's class, Seth had probed the secrets of the skies, peering through the lens his professor had brought back from Germany. Years after he'd forgotten some of his university studies, Seth remembered Professor Mitchel's astronomy lectures. His knowledge of the universe helped Seth keep perspective at this time when his life and the life of his nation hung in the balance.

A bright streak appeared in the sky, flared briefly, and then faded. A falling star, most people would call it. Seth knew better, but he felt a chill of apprehension each time he witnessed the phenomenon. In popular belief, a falling star foretold death or disaster, but his education had kept him from confusing the science of astronomy with the ignorance of superstition.

"The heavens declare the handiwork of God," he recalled hearing his mother read. He did not have her faith, but with that much he could agree. Seth sighed. He had just turned thirty, yet he felt almost old, aware that his life so far hadn't amounted to very much. He had spent years completing his education and beginning his law practice, a life that had been safe, profitable—and lonely.

Seth glanced at the stars once more before lowering the sash. Somewhere there might be someone he could love and who would love him in return. Someday, no thanks to the stars, they'd find each other. Someday. For the time being, though, Seth would serve his country.

March of 1862 arrived in northern Alabama with rain and raw winds that tore at the just-opened buttercups, pushing them to the earth and tattering their delicate golden fringes. Then in the quick change of the Southern spring, warm breezes and a bright sun coaxed the flowers to stand again, yellow splashes of color against the greening grass of early April.

Lucinda waited each year for the buttercups to bloom, taking their arrival as a signal that another dreary winter was at last over. Picking the first bouquet had become a special ritual, and this day Lucinda held each bloom to her face, savoring the fragrance.

So absorbed was Lucinda in her task that she didn't notice her father as he walked up Adams Street from his office. He stood at the gate for a moment, fondly watching his only daughter. She was slightly built, as her mother had been, although her mobile mouth and large, wide-set gray eyes more resembled her father's. Lucinda had a way of walking on tiptoe, as if afraid of missing something that taller people might see. Arnold Matthews often marveled at his daughter's enthusiasm and capacity for finding pleasure in the smallest things. These days, he thought as he opened the gate, there seemed to be precious few things to enjoy.

"Oh, hello, Papa. Look. Aren't these pretty?"

Lucinda held up her bouquet, inviting him to enjoy their aroma.

"Very nice," he said, wrinkling his nose, "but also a bit overpowering."

Lucinda thought her father looked distinguished and important, but too serious, and she liked to see his rare smile. His prematurely white hair and bright blue eyes added to his handsome appearance, and Lucinda thought it was no wonder that half the widows in Huntsville had set their caps for him. So far none had caught him.

"I wish Henry could be here to enjoy them with us," Lucinda said as they walked to the house. "Was there any news today?"

"Only that the Fourth Alabama did well in recent action around Yorktown. General Johnston himself singled them out for special honor."

"Is that all?" Lucinda asked, disappointed.

"No names were mentioned, if that's what you mean. On the other hand, there wasn't a casualty list with the dispatch, so we may assume that your brother is all right."

"I wish he'd write more often," Lucinda said.

"I doubt he's had much time. But if anything had happened to him, I'm sure we would be told."

As they entered the double front doors, Lige, their man-of-all-work, met them and took Lucinda's bouquet.

"Here, Lige, ask Viola to find a vase for these. They'd be nice on the dining room table."

"Yes'm. Afternoon, Mr. Matthews." Lige balanced Mr. Matthews's hat, walking stick, and topcoat in one hand and the flowers in the other as father and daughter left the foyer and entered the everyday sitting room to the left.

As were all the rooms in the house, the sitting room was spacious, with high ceilings and many windows. French doors led to a wide veranda where the family often spent the hottest summer days. On this March day, however, the doors were closed and a fire awaited kindling against the chill of evening.

The room's furnishings were more comfortable than elegant, in contrast to the mirror-image formal parlor on the other side of the hall. There the draperies and uphol-stery were brocade and velvet, and twin Aubusson rugs covered most of the parquet floor. The family sitting room, with its chintz and less-formal flowered carpet, was the comfortable heart of the house.

"I saw Charles Leonard this morning," Lucinda's father said as he settled into the overstuffed depths of his favorite chair.

"And?" Lucinda prompted when her father paused. Johnny Leonard was one of the younger members of Ben's company.

"He said there's a rumor that the boys have been moved up to southwest Tennessee. That's close enough so they might get to come home occasionally. I'm sure you'd be pleased to see your Lieutenant Bradley again."

"Ben's not *my* lieutenant," Lucinda replied, annoyed by her father's amused look.

"He seems to think so," her father began and might have said more, but the ringing of the small silver bell that called them to meals stopped him.

They entered the family dining room at the rear of the sitting room, where Lige, now wearing a white jacket, waited to seat them. Viola moved silently around the table, serving the succession of dishes that made up their largest meal of the day. Lucinda's buttercups sat in a crystal vase in the middle of the table, their fragrance competing with the pleasant odors of the roast chicken Viola had prepared.

"I've been considering asking your Aunt Millie to come for a visit," Arnold said as they ate.

"I hope she will," Lucinda said. She'd always loved her mother's older sister. "In fact, I wish she'd move to town."

"Well, there's no hope for that. Even with a good overseer and some of the best hands in Madison County, she thinks Highmeadows will fall apart if she's not there every minute."

"She might come for a little while, though."

"I'm sure she won't even consider leaving until after spring planting, but I'll write that you especially want to see her."

Lucinda thought of how she had once assumed that her father might marry Aunt Millie after Buck Sherrill's sudden death. The Old Testament was clear on the duty a man had to take care of his kin. But to Lucinda and Henry's disappointment, neither their aunt nor their father had seemed interested in merging their households.

"I'll be heading back to town," Mr. Matthews said a few minutes later as he pushed his chair away from the table. "And what are your plans?"

"I'm taking my sewing to Alice Ann's," Lucinda replied, following her father into the hall.

"You two stay inside entirely too much," her father observed. "In this fine weather you ought to spend some time outdoors."

"And get all sunburned and freckled?" Lucinda asked in mock horror.

"Oh, yes," Arnold said fondly, "I sometimes forget that you're now a grand lady in long skirts."

"Well, I am, and when Alice Ann and I start teaching in the primary school in September, we'll have to act very grownup."

"In the meantime, you shouldn't behave like old spinsters."

"We don't have much choice about that, but having Aunt Millie here would help. Don't forget to write to her," Lucinda said as her father left. Then she called to Viola, "I'm going to the Allison's house now. I'll be home before supper."

"You'd better, less'n I has to send after you again,"
Viola replied crossly. Her overprotective manner annoyed
Lucinda, but next to her own family and Alice Ann, she felt
closest to Viola, and she smiled at the wiry black woman
as she left.

The Allisons lived on Greene Street, diagonally behind
and barely in sight of the Matthews' house. Although they
were quite different, Alice Ann and Lucinda had grown up
as best friends. Lucinda was fair and lively, with an
impetuous streak, while Alice Ann was dark and more
inclined to be serious. The girls had planned to take a grand
tour of Europe the previous June after having been grad-
uated from the Huntsville Female Seminary. War had
cancelled their trip, probably permanently. Now, instead
of the fancy work they had learned at school, the girls
stitched plain lawn and muslin shirts for the Ladies
Humane Society to send to Confederate soldiers they'd
never meet.

As they worked, the girls talked, re-hashing every scrap
of news until it was quite worn out. On this afternoon,
Alice Ann's mother, whom Lucinda called Aunt Dora and
regarded as a second mother, joined them in the Allisons'
cozy sewing room.

"Is there any news of Henry?" Aunt Dora asked as she
always did, and as she usually had to, Lucinda shook her
head.

"No, and it's almost two months since his last letter.
Papa heard that the Fourth Alabama had been commended
for work near Yorktown."

Dora Allison sighed and shook her head. "This war was
a terrible mistake. Your brother and our Aaron could
hardly wait to get into it, and now a day never passes that

I don't wear out my knees praying that somehow they'll live through it."

"At least you've seen Aaron," Lucinda said. "If Henry's had a furlough, he's been too far away to get home."

"But Henry doesn't have a wife waiting for him, as our Aaron does," Alice Ann added. Sally Merrick had married Aaron just before the war began. She now lived with her parents and sometimes joined the girls' sewing sessions.

There was silence, then Lucinda spoke. "I almost forgot—Papa is going to ask Aunt Millie to visit us after spring planting."

"Oh? How is your aunt these days?" Mrs. Allison asked.

"All right, I suppose. We haven't heard from her lately."

"Millie should have found a tenant for that place and moved to town years ago. Heaven only knows what might lurk out there in the country these days. Arnold should have made her leave when Buck Sherrill died," Dora Allison declared.

"Papa tried to persuade Aunt Millie to do that—he even found a tenant for her—but she won't leave the place. She's set on keeping it going until she can hand it over to Henry, and she's convinced things won't go right if she leaves."

"Well, that could be the truth, but Millie's always been plumb pig-headed, anyway," Mrs. Allison said shortly. She stood and brushed lint from her dress. "I'm going to see to supper now," she said. "Don't you girls sit out here and strain your eyes when the light fades. Ask Mandy to bring you a lamp."

"We will," Alice Ann promised. As soon as her mother left the room, she put down the shirt she had been stitching and sighed. "That was mean, what Mama said about Aunt

Millie. I hope she'll come here."

"So do I," Lucinda said. "And by the way, Papa said the Huntsville Rifles might be up in Tennessee now. Since they're so close, maybe we'll see some of them soon."

Alice Ann put down her sewing and grinned at Lucinda. "Ben Bradley, you mean!"

"Well, yes, and the others too, of course."

"How many others did you kiss goodbye in the middle of the depot?" Alice Ann asked. She hadn't been anywhere near Lucinda and Ben that afternoon, but she'd heard about it and liked to tease Lucinda about what she called her "great farewell scene."

"It seems that everybody in town knows about my kissing," Lucinda grumbled. "Ben would probably be humiliated if he knew we were talking about him like this."

"Oh, I doubt it," said Alice Ann. "I just wish someone special was thinking about me."

"And I wish we didn't have to make these shirts," Lucinda said.

"When this war is over, I solemnly vow that I will never put a needle to another shirt as long as I live!" Alice Ann declared.

"Amen to that!" rejoined Lucinda.

For the rest of the afternoon the girls worked on in comfortable silence, each thinking of the magic days when the war would be over, the boys would come back home, and everything would be as it had been before.

Major Seth Russell swiveled in his saddle and looked back at the infantry troops that snaked out behind him in a long, wavering line. The men were tired and rations were short, but their morale continued to be high as they marched along the back roads of Middle Tennessee, headed back to their encampment at Murfreesboro.

They had good cause to be cheerful, Seth thought. In the few short months the Third Division of the Fourth Ohio, Brigadier General O. M. Mitchel, commanding, had been in the field, it had successfully taken town after town while suffering only light casualties. Their first objective, Bowling Green, Kentucky, had been abandoned before they even got there. Then they'd moved on to Nashville, where the mayor had come out under a flag of truce and surrendered the city without a shot fired.

Everything has gone too well, Seth thought. Something bad was bound to happen to them sooner or later.

"I guess we showed Morgan he can't get by with raiding our forage wagons," a young lieutenant said as he rode up beside Seth. They had just chased away some Confederates who'd tried to take their provisions.

"I hope so. We need all the food we can get."

Maintaining troops hundreds of miles inside enemy territory—for that was what the Confederate States now were—had created the biggest headaches for the invaders. Along with being made General Mitchel's adjutant, Seth had been assigned to keep the men and their animals fed and supplied as they traveled, a task that became ever more difficult.

"I thought we were going to join General Buell and invade Mississippi," the lieutenant said. "Now that Nashville's secure, it would seem a likely course, don't you agree?"

Seth shrugged in reply. He had no intention of discussing military matters with Lieutenant Stryker, who had grown a scraggly beard in an effort to appear older but still reminded Seth of a boy playing at war.

"The Army of Ohio's the only major federal command that's never fought a real battle on its own. What is General Buell waiting for?" Stryker persisted.

"Whatever it is, I'm willing to leave it to the generals, and I suggest that you do the same," Seth said. He spurred his horse on, leaving the lieutenant to eat his dust.

Reaching their temporary camp, Seth went directly to brigade headquarters where the general was waiting for him. General Mitchel was a rather imposing man, clean-shaven and thin-lipped, with a high forehead and bristling eyebrows over piercing eyes.

"How did your operation go?"

"Very well, sir. We found our forage train and retook it, along with eight Rebel horses. John Morgan won't try that maneuver again."

"Good," General Mitchel said, but Seth saw that he seemed preoccupied. "We have more pressing concerns now. A courier just brought this." The general handed Seth a telegraph message.

"Enemy fully engaged near Pittsburg Landing," he read aloud.

"Another battle without our part of the Army of Ohio," General Mitchel fumed.

"Where is this Pittsburg Landing?" Seth asked. General Mitchel unrolled a map and pointed.

"In Tennessee, north of Corinth. Grant has been waiting there a month for Buell and the Army of the Ohio to join him for the attack on Mississippi."

"The Confederates must have started it, then? I suppose it's too far away for us to join the fighting."

General Mitchel nodded. "Yes, but we have other plans." He moved his finger east of Corinth to a dot near the Tennessee River.

"Huntsville, Alabama? What's there?" Seth asked.

"The hub of the Memphis and Charleston Railroad that supplies the Confederacy. With it in our hands, their supplies will be cut off—and we can use the rail lines to resupply our troops."

"Is the place well-fortified?" Seth asked, thinking that such a strategic location must surely be heavily defended.

"Our intelligence says not, but I'm sending out scouts tomorrow to make sure."

"And then?"

The general rolled up the map and put it back in its case. "We'll go there and take it. Make sure every man rests well for the next few days. It might be their last chance for a while."

On Sunday, Lucinda and her father walked to church, enjoying the fine weather. The Presbyterian Church was already half-filled, and they nodded to acquaintances as they made their way to their family pew. Everyone knew Arnold Matthews, who served as an elder and had always furnished generous financial support.

"I see Charles Clemons," Lucinda's father said as they sat down. "After services we must ask if he knows any more about Henry's regiment."

Lucinda turned and nodded to the Clemons family. Looking about, she noted that there were very few gray uniforms in evidence. A year earlier, some four thousand men had been quartered in Huntsville awaiting provisions, but now, except for a small garrison guarding the Charleston and Memphis Railroad depot and yards, no Confederates were stationed there.

Lucinda saw Ollice Kinnard, his right sleeve hanging slack and empty from a wagon accident. *Surely he'll be mustered out now,* she thought. Will Hinkle had managed to get a furlough and was sitting with Dolly Harris, who looked like a cat with a bowl of cream. Will had always been sweet on Dolly, and Lucinda guessed that they would soon announce their engagement—or there might be a hasty marriage—before Will rejoined his unit.

The service began, and as Pastor Ross prayed, Lucinda added silent petitions for her brother, her family, and their friends. It didn't occur to her that thousands of similar prayers were being offered in the North. She hadn't the slightest doubt that the Lord was on their side, would help them win, and would sustain them in the meantime.

After the service, the churchyard quickly filled with knots of conversing groups. Almost universally, the topic was the war—its progress and the whereabouts of local troops. Seeing the Bradleys in conversation near the Clemons family, Lucinda edged close enough to hear what they were saying, while also listening to Mr. Clemons' reply to her father about the regiment in which both Eddie Clemons and Henry served.

"No, we've heard nothing from Ben lately, but we expect. . . ."

The rest of the sentence was lost as Mr. Clemons said, "Eddie doesn't write, either, but Will Hinkle says the boys are fine and he thinks the whole unit may be furloughed soon."

"I pray that he's right," Arnold said.

Ben's parents were talking to Ollice Kinnard, and while

Lucinda wanted to ask about Ben, she didn't want to interrupt them.

"Shall we go now?" Mr. Matthews asked, offering Lucinda his arm. They had just crossed Gates Street when Lucinda heard her name called.

"Miss Lucinda! I almost forgot to give this to you."

She turned and stopped when she saw Ollice Kinnard.

"Hello, Ollice. I'm sorry about your. . .ah. . .your accident."

"Thanks." He ducked his head in embarrassment and handed Lucinda a dirty envelope, crudely sealed with candle wax and bearing her name.

"When did you get this?" she asked, not having to ask from whom it had come. Seeing the handwriting, she felt her heart tighten.

"Lieutenant Bradley gave it to me when he heard I was comin' home. He asked me to see that you got it in person, and this is the first chance I've had. Must be two weeks, now. I kind of lost track of time there for a while," he added apologetically.

"I can see why," Mr. Matthews said. "Are you home to stay now?"

"Prob'ly, sir. Mama says she won't let me go back even if they'd have me. I reckon I'll be helping Pa in the hardware store."

"Thank you for bringing the letter," Lucinda said.

"I wish we'd get a letter from Henry," Mr. Matthews said as they resumed walking. "But if the Clemons' news is correct, perhaps he'll finally get that furlough, after all." Then, glancing at Lucinda and seeing that she had not opened her letter, he smiled faintly. "Go ahead and open it. I promise not to read over your shoulder."

"I'll wait," Lucinda replied, the color rising in her cheeks.

Only when she was safely back in her own room did Lucinda break the seal and read Ben's letter.

two

Dear Miss Lucinda,

I may see you soon! I don't know exactly when, but we are close to Huntsville and will be even closer, they say. This winter was long and hard, with a lot more waiting than anything. There's a big fight coming soon, and we'll be part of it. I am more convinced than ever that we will win this war and, pray God, be home to stay soon. I still have what you gave me, and I carry it all the time. Ollice is waiting for me, and I must write my parents. How I long to see you all again! Until then, I remain Yr. ob'd't servant,

Benjamin S. Bradley, CSA.
P. S. I'm now a first lieutenant.

Lucinda read the letter several times, almost expecting more words to appear, feeling after the last reading that she knew little more than she had before the first. Ben had said he hoped to come home, but Lucinda wondered if that were merely wishful thinking. The talk about the big fight they were expecting was somewhat disturbing, yet she knew that every battle fought and won would speed the day when Ben and her brother and everyone else would be free to come home for good.

With a sigh, Lucinda added the note to the others he had sent her over the past few months. She looked at the small store of letters and tried to recollect their writer's features, but even when she closed her eyes and thought hard, Ben's face seemed an uncertain blur, like a bad watercolor portrait left out in a rain shower. She wished he'd given her his ambrotype to remember him by. But, Lucinda thought, if he came home soon and they could again meet face-to-face, she would be able to tell what was actual from her dreams.

On Friday, Aunt Millie's man Rufe came to Huntsville for supplies and brought her answer to Arnold's invitation.

"Come in and let Viola give you some lunch," Lucinda told Rufe as she took Millie's letter. "I have some things to send to Highmeadows."

"Yes'm, I'll be glad to do that. You comin' to see us agin this summer, Miss Lucinda?"

"Perhaps, Rufe, if I'm invited."

The old slave's face lit up as he smiled, showing several gaps where teeth were missing. "Miss Millie, she'll ask, no doubt 'bout dat. She tole me today, 'Rufe, you tell Miss Lucinda we want her to come to see us,' and I tole her, 'Yes'm, I shorely will.'"

Lucinda smiled at the old man's way of embellishing Aunt Millie's words. "We'll see, Rufe. Now go on and find Viola while I see what Mrs. Sherrill has to say."

The news was disappointing. Aunt Millie wrote that she couldn't consider coming for a visit in the near future. The letter ended with a discouraging phrase: "Under the present circumstances, I must stay here."

As Lucinda gathered things to send to Highmeadows, she wondered what her aunt could mean by her remark. When she gave Rufe the basket, she asked him if there had been any problems at the plantation.

"No'm, I reckon not," Rufe replied, but Lucinda noticed that he and Lige had exchanged a peculiar look when she'd asked the question, and they appeared to whisper together before Rufe took his leave.

"I doubt if anything is wrong," Arnold assured her when Lucinda told him about the incident that evening. "I'm sorry Millie feels she can't come, but I'm not really surprised. Perhaps you and Alice Ann might go to Highmeadows for a visit, instead."

"I wouldn't want to abandon you," Lucinda said, half-seriously.

"I'm quite certain that I can manage without you, as I probably must do when your young lieutenant comes home."

"Don't tease me about Ben," Lucinda said, and something in her voice must have warned her father, for he did not try to answer her. "We have more important things to worry about, I mean," she added.

Lucinda went to bed at her usual hour that night, but she lay awake for a long time, wishing that Ben would come home, that *something* exciting would happen to help the time pass more quickly.

Be careful what you wish for, she thought, remembering something she had once heard, *you might get it.* Finally, she fell asleep.

"It's two o'clock, Major," a voice warned, and Seth struggled awake. He hadn't meant to sleep at all, but the relentless march of the past two days had taken its toll.

"Thanks, Corporal." Seth stretched and then stood, his few hours' sleep having made him feel somewhat rested. They had halted ten miles south of Fayetteville, Tennessee, at dusk, having covered forty miles in forty hours. Another four hours of steady marching would bring them to Huntsville and the headquarters of the Memphis and Charleston Railroad.

Seth splashed water from his canteen on his face and wished he could shave. This march afforded no time for such frills, and he would have to enter Huntsville with the stubble of three days' beard. It was one of the many hardships he had somehow failed to anticipate.

"Silent march, ho!"

The order was almost whispered down the line, as the Fourth Ohio Cavalry, the Eighth Brigade, and Simonson's battery began to move. No one spoke, and everything possible had been done to reduce the noise from clanking mess kits and the jingling harnesses on the mules pulling the supply wagons.

Thousands of stars shone, helping the troops to find their way as they moved steadily south past several imposing plantation homes. Seth looked up at the sky, where meteors continued to shower from the radiance of Leo at the rate of some ten an hour. Soon the stars would fade as the earth turned to meet the sun and their march reached its appointed end.

"What do you suppose we'll find there?" Lieutenant Stryker whispered to Seth.

"People," he replied. Civilians, not soldiers, they thought, but they didn't know for sure. They didn't even know whether the fighting at Pittsburg Landing had ended or with what result. At last report, the Confederates were winning an engagement at a place called Shiloh Church. While that battle might still be going on, General Mitchel was leading his men ever deeper into enemy territory, truly on their own.

Seth swallowed hard. He felt an edge of impatience to find out what awaited them. Whatever it was, he was ready for it.

Lucinda's rest was disturbed by troubled dreams, so that at first she thought she was hearing shouting in a nightmare. But when she opened her eyes in the half-light of the dawn of April 11, she realized the sounds were only too real.

Going to the front window of her bedroom, Lucinda looked out to see many of the neighbors standing in the street and gazing toward the downtown area. Lige came around the house, talked with the Allison's houseman, and ran back inside. He called loudly to Viola, and his words were so ridiculous that Lucinda could scarcely believe them.

"The Yankees is come! They done got the railroad!"

It can't be true, Lucinda told herself as she hastily dressed and joined the knot of people in the street. She listened intently to the scraps of conversation, each detail adding to her grim realization that something truly horrifying had taken place.

"There must be thousands of them, blue uniforms swarming everywhere you look. . . ."

"They captured the rolling stock and a hospital train. . . ."

"Took a bunch of prisoners. . . ."

"No, there wasn't any warning at all. . . ."

Lucinda turned to see Lige beside her. "You'd best stay in the house, Missy," Lige warned.

"Have you seen Papa?" she asked.

"Yes'm, he downtown now. Don't you worry none," he

said, and Lucinda reluctantly left the street and went inside, casting a last look in the direction of the depot as if she could somehow see it through an act of will. Lucinda stood tensely at the front windows. She wished that her father hadn't rushed off to see what was happening, and that she had the freedom to go, too—a freedom that men took for granted.

> *Message to General Lorenzo Thomas, Adjutant-General, Headquarters Nashville, from Brigadier-General Ormsby M. Mitchel:*
>
> *After a forced march of incredible difficulty, leaving Fayetteville yesterday at 12 noon, my advanced guard, consisting of Turchin's brigade, Kennett's cavalry, and Simonson's battery, entered Huntsville this morning at six o'clock. The city was taken completely by surprise, no one having considered the march practicable in the time. We have captured about two hundred prisoners, fifteen locomotives, a large amount of passenger and box cars, the telegraph office and apparatus, and two Southern mails. We have at length succeeded in cutting the great artery of railway communication between the Southern states.*
>
> *O. M. Mitchel, Brigadier-Gen'l, Commanding*

"That ought to please Mr. Lincoln," observed Captain Warren, reading aloud a copy of the dispatch.

"Taking is one thing—holding will be another," said Seth Russell. It was his job to find billets for the officers, and turning civilians out of their homes was one duty which he didn't relish.

"Oh, we'll keep it, no doubt about that!" Captain Warren exclaimed. "We'll keep it!"

In a rough camp they'd made across from the depot, Seth managed to shave, wash, and put on a fresh shirt. "You, Lieutenant Stryker, and I will form patrols and procure housing," Seth directed the captain.

No matter how distasteful they were, Seth had orders to carry out.

An hour later, Lucinda's father returned, his face drawn. He tried to sound reassuring, but it was evident that the sudden federal onslaught had been a heavy blow to him.

"It is absolutely incredible that eight thousand troops could just march in and take over without the slightest warning," he fumed.

"There are that many?" Lucinda asked, her eyes widening.

"That's what their commander, a General Mitchel, says. Of course, he's probably overstating the case, but from the blue uniforms I saw swarming through the streets, I don't doubt his word. He was really proud to capture the Memphis and Charleston Railroad with so little resistance."

"Is that why they came—for the railroad?"

"Yes. They want to cut the supply route between the western Confederacy and our soldiers in Virginia."

"Like Henry and Aaron," Lucinda said. "What will happen now?" She thought of the vague stories of atrocities in other cities and shivered.

"No one knows, but for now they've declared martial law and set up a military government."

"Maybe if the railroad is all they want, they won't stay long," Lucinda said, realizing even as she spoke that it was wishful thinking.

Her father shook his head and took both her hands in his. "I have no answers, Lucinda. But I want you to stay inside the house, and if anyone comes when I'm not here, let Lige or Viola deal with them. Is that clear?"

Lucinda nodded and tried to speak, but a knot filled her throat. From his tone, she knew her father feared for her safety.

"It'll be all right," he added, clumsily patting her arm as he used to do when she was a small child frightened by a storm. "God will take care of us."

"I know." Lucinda backed away and made herself as tall as she could, determined not to cry.

"I must go back downtown—I'll be back soon."

After her father left, Lucinda thought about what might happen, not only to them, but to their soldiers who might be trying to come home on furlough. If they didn't know that Huntsville was in federal hands, they might become prisoners of war in their own home town. *Keep them safe, Lord,* she prayed.

Almost immediately, Lucinda saw her first Union soldiers. She stood behind the lace curtains in the family sitting room and watched them pass, curious to see the face of the enemy. The federal troops didn't look as polished as she had expected them to. Perhaps because they had just traveled for hours on a forced march, most of the men were tired and dirty. She saw some soldiers older than her father and others who looked younger than her brother. All carried carbines with fixed bayonets, but Lucinda was somewhat comforted by the thought that they looked more tired than threatening.

By mid-afternoon, troops passed only occasionally, and Lucinda had just decided to abandon her post when she realized that one group of soldiers had stopped at her front gate.

An unmounted officer—Lucinda identified him as such by his military bearing and the sword at his side— accompanied by five enlisted men surveyed the Matthews' house for a moment before he opened the gate and started up the walk. When the officer looked directly at the window where she stood, Lucinda saw a dark haired, clean-shaven man with a handsome face, a man who looked accustomed to having his orders obeyed.

Had he noticed her watching him? For a moment he slowed his pace, and Lucinda stepped away from the window. Then, with no change in his expression, he moved on. A moment later the heavy brass door knocker resounded through the house. Lucinda stayed where she was as Lige went to the door. She heard the federal officer ask to speak to the head of the house.

"Mr. Matthews be downtown," Lige replied, sounding unafraid. Lucinda wondered what Lige really thought about the Yankees.

"I have orders to inspect this house," the officer said, and before Lige could make any reply, the soldiers pushed past him and came inside.

Lucinda ran into the hall and faced the man who had given the orders to search her home.

"May I ask what you are looking for?" she asked. The men turned to stare at her.

"Pardon the intrusion, ma'am," the officer said, bowing slightly. "I am Major Russell, adjutant to General Mitchel.

I have orders to search for hidden arms and Rebel soldiers. We're also requisitioning suitable houses for our use."

Apparently not expecting Lucinda to reply, he turned away and with a nod directed his men to begin their work.

An emotion she had never before experienced overwhelmed Lucinda, more than fear or anger, but with overtones of both. Her cheeks were flaming, and her fists were so tightly clenched that her fingernails dug into the flesh of her palms. *Help me, God,* she prayed silently. When she spoke again, her voice was firm and clear.

"We have neither weapons nor soldiers, Major. You are wasting your time in this house."

Major Russell did not reply, but began to walk through the downstairs rooms, Lucinda following close behind him. Viewing her home as she thought the major must, Lucinda saw the sterling silver tea service in the formal dining room, the Sevres porcelain on the parlor mantel, the ivory carvings in the sitting room. The major seemed to be making a mental inventory of every room through which they passed. His face remained expressionless as he walked up the curving staircase and began to tour the upstairs.

Lucinda tried to match her stride to his, but soon fell behind. A soldier emerged from Henry's room with the old musket that her brother sometimes used for hunting. Another had found the matched set of duelling pistols, never fired, which had belonged to Lucinda's grandfather.

"So there are no weapons in the house?" the major said, looking levelly at Lucinda. "And what about the owner of this?"

Henry's clothes press had yielded his dress gray uniform, left behind when his unit exchanged farewell balls for fighting.

"I don't know," Lucinda replied quietly. The sight of Henry's uniform reminded her of their precarious position, but she held her head high and locked gazes with the Major. "We have neither seen nor heard from my brother for a long time. He is certainly not in this house."

An expression that Lucinda could not decipher passed fleetingly over the major's face, and he was the first to look away. Without comment, he turned aside and called to the patrol to search the grounds and servants' quarters. With a brief glance at Lucinda's room and the unused fourth bedroom, he started down the stairs. Lucinda winced as the sword at his side hit against the banisters with every step. If the federals took over their house, nothing they had would be safe.

"Miss. . .," the Major began, looked at the list he was holding, and added, "Matthews?" When she nodded, his brown eyes gave her a long, searching look, and this time it was she who looked away. It seemed a long time before he spoke again. "I will tell General Mitchel that this house is unsuited for our needs. Of course, I can't guarantee that the general will agree. But for the present, you may remain."

Lucinda, who had been standing with her hands clasped in an unconscious attitude of prayer, brought them to her cheeks at his words, then quickly recovered. She was determined not to express gratitude for something that was no more than their due.

"Then I will bid you good day, major."

The major nodded curtly. His face was an expressionless mask, except for a tiny twitch of the muscles around his mouth, as if he were fighting a smile. Then, with another half-bow, he was gone.

Lucinda ran to the back veranda and looked out to see Lige and Viola standing silently in the rear yard, watching the major's soldiers peer inside their quarters and search through the carriage house. One of the men asked if they knew where any Rebel soldiers were, and both shook their heads.

Soon the major called to his men, and they gathered around him in the front of the house. Lucinda went to the sitting room window and watched their intruder consult his list, then signal the patrol to move on to the next house. Before they left, he looked back at the Matthews' house for a long moment, as if to mark it for future reference. Then he, too, moved on, and Lucinda felt a surge of relief.

"Lordy mercy, Miss Lucinda," Viola cried as she came into the sitting room. "That sure was a pryin' lot o' men. Did they bother you any, child?"

"No, they didn't," Lucinda replied, turning from the window with the best attempt at a smile she could muster. "The Yankee major took some of our things, but he said we could stay."

"Praise de Lord!" Viola muttered.

Lucinda thought of the way the officer had looked at her and wondered fleetingly if she had read him correctly. Had she not been there, Lucinda was almost certain that the major wouldn't have let them stay. Then she had the nagging thought that the general might not be quite so generous as his adjutant. In any case, Lucinda's fears about life under a military occupation had been confirmed; nothing could be taken for granted.

The soldiers had been gone only a short time when Alice Ann came to the french doors at the side of the sitting room.

"Oh, Lucinda, it's so awful!" she exclaimed, and burst into tears.

The girls embraced and Lucinda led Alice Ann to the sofa, where Viola set about using smelling salts, a damp cloth, and a great deal of petting and murmuring to calm Alice Ann.

"I can't stay," Alice Ann said when she could speak again. "The Yankees ordered us to be out of our house by sundown!"

"I'm so sorry," Lucinda replied, squeezing Alice Ann's hand. In her relief at being allowed to stay in her home, Lucinda hadn't stopped to consider that their friends might not be so fortunate. "What will you do?"

"Papa says we can go to the country place in Limestone County. The house isn't very large, but Mama sent me to ask if you all wanted to go with us. I don't guess you need to, though," she added forlornly.

"We've been allowed to stay, at least for now," Lucinda replied. "But how can you be ready to leave by sundown? That's ridiculous."

"We're only taking a few things. We have to be out today."

"We'll help you, then," Lucinda said, rising.

"You shouldn't leave your house unguarded," Alice Ann warned. "I saw the way they looked at our things. There won't be anything left if the Yankees get hold of it."

"Then we'll bring your valuables over here. Viola, you stay here and tell Lige to come with me."

At the Allisons' house, people were running in all directions, a rapidly growing stock of boxes and trunks by the carriage house evidence of their industry. Mrs. Allison came over to the girls, shaking her head.

"We'll never get half of that into our wagon," she declared.

"You can use our carriage," Lucinda volunteered. "Lige can drive it for you and bring it back tomorrow."

"Thank you, my dear, but we can't possibly get anywhere this evening."

"Then you must stay with us tonight," Lucinda said firmly. "Now tell me what I can take to our house for safekeeping."

By the time the Allisons' luggage had been stowed in the wagons inside their locked carriage house and their more portable valuables had been taken to the Matthews' house, darkness had fallen, and they were all tired.

Supper was hastily assembled by Viola and the Allisons' cook, and while they ate, the families listened as Mr. Allison and Mr. Matthews reported on what was happening downtown, where the men had been most of the day. Although her father and Frank Allison tried to make light of the martial law regulations that the federals had imposed, Lucinda saw the looks that they exchanged and she guessed that they knew more than they were willing to tell the women.

"Mrs. Bradford and several other ladies have been caring for our wounded that were on the train the federals captured," Mr. Allison said.

"Poor fellows—to be delivered from a bloody battle, only to fall into enemy hands right here in our town," Lucinda's father added.

"Were any of them local boys?" she asked, thinking of Ben, who had written about expecting to be in a big fight.

"I don't think so. If they were, I'm sure the federals wouldn't have let the ladies see them. The men were on their way to the Confederate Hospital in Chattanooga. Some aren't so badly wounded."

"I wish I could help them," Aunt Dora said wearily. "I won't be any earthly use to anyone, 'way off in Limestone."

"This occupation may only be temporary," her husband said. "Now that they have the railroad, they'll probably just leave a small force to guard it and go on elsewhere."

"Then why are they moving into our house?" Alice Ann asked.

"They have to have some place to put their officers," Mr. Matthews replied. "I heard that the McDowell house is going to be General Mitchel's headquarters. Ours could be next, for all we know."

"From what Lucinda tells us, you have already been spared eviction," Aunt Dora said.

"What?" Arnold exclaimed, and Lucinda quickly told him about her encounter with the Yankee major.

"You mean there were troops in this house—and you talked to them? Why didn't you tell me this before?" he asked when she finished.

"I didn't have a chance. I'm sorry, Papa, but if I hadn't spoken up, we might be leaving, too. The major took Henry's musket and Grandpa's duelling pistols, but he was in control of his men. We were never in any danger."

"I wish we'd had such an officer at our house!" Aunt Dora exclaimed. "Some childish lieutenant was ordering all of us around like a second Napoleon. Such rudeness! I just know they'll ruin everything in the house," she added, and began to cry.

"Be that as it may," Arnold said, "the fact remains that this federal officer violated our privacy and took our

property. What's to keep him from changing his mind
about the house?"

"He said he couldn't guarantee that General Mitchel
wouldn't want the house anyway, but I believe he meant
it when he said we could stay."

"Very well, but I repeat that you are not to speak to any
federal officer or soldier or to let anyone enter this house.
Is that clear?"

He was wearing his best stern-Papa look, so Lucinda
looked down and barely nodded her assent. She knew he
only wanted to protect her. And of course the federals were
their enemies. Yet even as she agreed, Lucinda could not
wholeheartedly accept her father's order. If she hadn't
stood up to the major, they'd probably not have a roof over
their head now. In the future if circumstances made it
necessary, she'd do whatever she had to to keep their home
secure.

Alice Ann was so tired from the events of the day that
she fell asleep almost as soon as she had climbed into
Lucinda's four-poster bed. Lucinda, although tired in
body, was too keyed up to sleep. After lying awake and
wide-eyed for what seemed to be hours, she got out of bed
and went to her side window. She could barely make out
the McDowell house, screened by the intervening trees
that were almost in full leaf. There seemed to be quite a lot
of activity at the new federal headquarters, with soldiers
coming and going and light showing from several windows.

Major Russell is probably there right now, Lucinda
thought. *He's a Yankee, and they're evil and horrid and
the sooner they leave, the better.*

He had looked into her eyes and allowed her to stay in

her house. Might he not expect something in exchange for what he probably viewed as an act of extreme generosity?

Oh, Ben, Lucinda cried silently. *If only you were still here and the war hadn't happened. . . .*

Lucinda was too tired to finish her thought.

three

Seth Russell had never felt more tired than he did that night as he returned to the house that served as General Mitchel's headquarters.

"This sure beats a bivouac in the mud and cold," Captain Warren said, spreading his bedroll atop a patterned Brussels carpet in the McDowells' parlor. "I'd just as soon live here, myself."

"We can't," Seth replied. "The general wants to use this house strictly as his headquarters. Tomorrow we'll have to decide on a house for ourselves and get more beds moved."

"If I'd wanted to run a hotel, I wouldn't have made a soldier," Captain Warren grumbled.

"I know," Seth agreed. "But did you notice how pretty this area is, with the mountains all around it?"

Captain Warren snorted. "Pretty! No, I can't say as I did. But I noticed that some of the houses hereabouts are really elegant. No telling what kind of money's in this town."

"I hope there won't be any looting," Seth said, suddenly uneasy.

"Or shooting," Warren murmured as he pulled off his boots with a sigh of relief. "Maybe that'll be one good thing about this place."

I know another, Seth thought. All that day he had kept picturing the petite young woman who had stood up to him in her front hall. She had been so beautiful in her anger that Seth had allowed his judgment to be impaired. He should

42

have taken her house—it had four large bedrooms and was just a stone's throw from headquarters—but when he'd looked into her burning gray eyes, he couldn't order her out of her home.

You're a weak man, Major, Seth told himself, aware that he had no shield for that sort of weakness. But at least he knew her last name and where she lived. In time, he would see her again.

The Allisons left just after dawn the next morning, and as they waved goodbye, Lucinda knew that it could be a very long while until they met again. At the last minute it was decided that the Allisons should keep the Matthews' carriage in the country, where it would be safer from the federals. Lucinda watched them leave, sad but dry-eyed in the face of Alice Ann's tears.

After the Allisons left, Lucinda stayed inside behind drawn draperies, aware of the rumble of passing wagons and the shouts of federal troops moving into the houses that had been hastily vacated by their owners. Most of their neighbors' homes had been taken. The Matthews' house and a few smaller ones had become islands in an almost overwhelming sea of blue. As streams of soldiers thronged the streets, Adams Street resembled a Union barracks, with the federal or unit flags flying from most of the residences.

Torn between staying home with Lucinda and wanting to know what was happening to his business, Arnold finally went back to town after Lucinda assured him that she would be perfectly safe at home alone. However, she could not ignore the throngs of troops filling their once-tranquil street. She kept a fearful watch, expecting every passing group to enter and commandeer their house and praying they would not.

Finally, Lucinda went up to her room, where she read a few Psalms and asked God to keep Ben safe. She knew that his unit had probably been in the thick of the fighting at Shiloh and that massive Union forces had inflicted heavy Confederate casualties. For the first time Lucinda began to realize that she might never see Ben again.

"No!" she exclaimed aloud, and as if to deny that possibility, she began a letter to him. Although there was no way to send it, merely writing to Ben had become a necessary act of faith.

Around noon, Lucinda went to the front window to watch for her father to come home for lunch. Instead, Lige came from the rear hall, a look of concern stamped on his face.

"Miss Lucinda, Massa Matthews ain't gwine ter be home to lunch today—the Yankees is talkin' to him an' some of the other gen'mens."

"Where are they?" Lucinda asked, not liking the sound of it.

"At the depot. I 'spect he'll be back soon," Lige added.

"Of course he will," Lucinda said, trying to convince herself that it was so. After all, it was logical that the federals would want to talk to the leaders of the community, and her father had important business and financial connections.

Although Lucinda told herself that there was no reason to worry, she began to be genuinely afraid when her father still hadn't returned by lamp-lighting time. She was pacing the floor, ready to go in search of him, when he finally came home.

"Are you all right? I was so worried when Lige said the Yankees had you."

"Of course," Mr. Matthews said, attempting a smile. But he looked tired, and his tone was serious as he related the day's events. "Our new neighbor, General Mitchel, had a dozen of us in for a talk. He reminded us that he is in charge now and will decide which businesses will be allowed to operate. He also accused us of supporting guerrilla activities. He said if the problems continued, we would all be arrested."

"Arrested!" Lucinda put a hand to her throat. "Who are these guerrillas? What are they doing that the federals think you can stop?"

"Don't be concerned about it," Mr. Matthews said quickly, seeing her stricken look. "They must try to humble us, of course. They have the notion that someone in Huntsville is directing these men who fire into the Union trains and cut the telegraph wires and fire at stray federal soldiers."

"But that isn't true, is it?"

"Of course not. No one knows who the guerrillas are, but it's likely that most of them are either Confederate soldiers not presently part of a unit or local men defending their property. Even if I could, I wouldn't tell a soldier not to resist the enemy they have taken an oath to fight. I believe the others there today feel the same."

"Thank you for telling me the truth," Lucinda said.

"And when have I ever lied to you, young lady?" her father asked, trying for a light touch, but not quite succeeding.

"You know what I mean, Papa," Lucinda said, looking levelly at him. "I'm not a child any more. I would resent being treated like one."

Mr. Matthews sighed. "If I could protect you from the world by keeping you ignorant, I suppose I would try to do so. I don't expect to be arrested, but if I am, you must go to Highmeadows. Now ask Lige to bring a basin of water to my room, then I'll take my supper."

After the first few days, the immediate shock of the occupation wore off and people began to emerge from their homes and attempt to go about their normal business. But things were far from normal, and the first time Lucinda left the house, with her father by her side and Viola a step behind, her heart sank at the sight of each Union soldier. At first, pickets had been posted on every street corner, but after a few days, the soldiers had been set to building fortifications around the depot and on Echols Hill. Only the key intersections and roads out of town were guarded.

On her first trip out of the house, Lucinda was escorted to the Female Seminary, where the ladies had set up an informal headquarters. They did what they could for the wounded Confederate soldiers who had been captured on the train. Most of the men had been hurt in the battle at Shiloh Church, near Corinth, Mississippi, and under the watchful eyes of the Union guards, they were allowed to receive food and nursing care from the Huntsville ladies. Meanwhile, the single women went to work making bandages.

"I wish Alice Ann had stayed here!" Rebecca Clemons said after greeting Lucinda. The Clemons' house, like the Matthews', had been spared by the federals, and like Lucinda, Rebecca Clemons had come to the seminary to help pass the time and share what little crumbs of knowledge each possessed.

"I miss Alice Ann, too," Lucinda replied. "I even miss those awful shirts we made."

"Now we're tearing sheets into bandages," Rebecca said, waving a hand toward a long table where several girls sat all but hidden behind heaps of white cotton goods. The girls seemed subdued and talked in low tones as if they feared being overheard by the guards at the door.

"I'm sure our troops are just waiting to come in and retake Huntsville," Grace Tazewell said.

"Wouldn't that mean a big fight?" Lucinda asked, trying to imagine what it would be like to live in the middle of a battlefield.

"Not necessarily. If enough soldiers came all at once, they could take the federals by surprise. My Papa says they'd have to surrender, just like we had to."

"They can't leave soon enough for me," Dolly Harris declared. "I've seen enough blue uniforms to last me a lifetime."

Lucinda remembered the last time she had seen Dolly and wondered if she knew where Will Hinkle was. Later, when the girls stopped to stretch and have a dipper of water from the bucket in the corner, Lucinda went to Dolly and asked her about Will.

Dolly's face colored and she shook her head, looking around as if afraid of something. "I've heard nothing since he left to return to his unit. If he got caught on the railroad, they could take him as a prisoner of war. And if he wasn't in uniform, he could be shot as a spy."

Although she spoke matter-of-factly, Dolly's words were chilling. Of course what she said was true: there were certain rules of war that both sides would observe. Lucinda thought of how hopeful Ben had seemed about coming home. Even if he had gotten away before the battle at Shiloh Church began, he must have heard of Huntsville's capture.

"Then there are the guerrillas," Dolly added. "They sure make the federals mad, even if it doesn't do much good otherwise."

"Have you seen any of the guerrillas?" Lucinda asked, and Dolly shook her head.

"They don't come to town, you know. We should get back to the table. Watch yourself," she added, dropping her voice. "Some of our fair sisters wonder why their houses were taken and ours weren't."

Dolly walked away before Lucinda could reply, and there was never another opportunity for them to talk privately that afternoon. But Lucinda understood what Dolly meant. The attentions of a federal officer, even though unwelcome, could be quite enough to estrange her from her friends.

That night when her father asked about her day, Lucinda told him they had discussed the guerrilla problem. "If these men aren't doing any good, it seems they'd stop their raids," Lucinda said.

"I'm sure they believe they are having some effect. Anyway, a soldier must fight in any way he can," her father replied. "I don't believe that our soldiers would knowingly make matters worse for us."

"But how could they know what effect their raids were having on the people in Huntsville?"

Mr. Matthews shrugged and shook his head, half-smiling. "You always did like to ask questions I couldn't answer. All I know is to pray that our military leaders will do the right thing—and that we will, as well."

"Do you think that Henry knows Huntsville has been occupied?"

"Another unanswerable question!"

"Then I'll ask an easy one. Shall we go to church tomorrow?"

"Yes, of course. This is the one Sunday we must never miss."

"It's a strange Easter we're observing this year," Lucinda said, feeling sad as she recalled other, happier Resurrection celebrations.

"Don't forget that Easter is about hope. God's still in charge—we must remind ourselves of that every day."

General Mitchel hadn't had a good week. Seth sat in his commander's office on Saturday, listening to him vent his ire.

Having heard nothing from his superior, General Don Carlos Buell, Mitchel had sent a dispatch to Secretary of War Stanton on Thursday, asking for more men to help defend his line of operations, which now extended from Tuscumbia east to Decatur. In reply, he had that day received a communication from General Buell to the effect that the Tennessee River bridges beyond Stevenson and at Decatur must be destroyed.

"How do they think we're going to be able to take Chattanooga and Knoxville without bridges to get us there?" General Mitchel demanded.

"I suppose it isn't in the master battle plan just now," Seth said, aware that his commander and General Buell had never gotten along well.

"If it's not, it ought to be!" the general exclaimed, scowling once more at Buell's message. "If they'd just send me some more men, I'd be able to take Chattanooga and go on to Knoxville, too."

Only after he had left the general's presence did Seth permit himself a small smile. It wasn't really funny, of course, for grown men—and generals, at that—to feud as Mitchel and Buell were doing, but it was rather interesting to see which side would win. If Mitchel got his way, a small garrison would be left to guard Huntsville, and the rest would once more be soldiering. The men had joined the army to fight, so most would welcome the opportunity. But if not. . . . *This isn't a bad place,* Seth thought, with a glance toward the Matthews' house.

Easter Sunday was flawlessly fair, the kind of day that only April can bring to northern Alabama. The golden forsythia and buttercups had given way to a varied palette of colors as azaleas, hawthorns, flowering crab, and peach trees were in full bloom. Early white and purple flags were out, and the lacy white dogwoods displayed their glory. But to Lucinda, the beauty of nature seemed almost a mockery, contrary as it was to conditions in Huntsville.

Arnold Matthews held his daughter's arm tightly as they walked past groups of federal soldiers that thronged the streets and lounged around the verandas of some of the occupied houses. The men laughed and talked loudly, and some called out as they passed.

"Hey, Missy Rebel! Where are ya' going so dressed up?"

"Wooee, look at the Sesech!"

Lucinda's cheeks flamed, more in anger than modesty, but she didn't look up. Acknowledging that she heard any group of men would not be ladylike. Not for any price

Please look up the following passage(s) and
read aloud when the passage is called for:

Mark 16:16

Thanks

would she respond to these raucous, uncouth enemies.

Her father's face reddened and he gripped her arm tightly. "Those men would do better to be in church," he observed as they reached the end of Adams Street and turned the corner. A few minutes later they entered the sanctuary, and Lucinda was made painfully aware of how much everything had changed. Only days ago she had received Ben's note, so full of hope that he would soon be home. Now she wondered if she would ever see him or her brother again.

The Bradley family pew was empty, along with several other pews. No gray uniforms were in evidence, of course, but with shock Lucinda saw that three federal officers were seated in the visitors' pew—including the major who had visited her house. After she was seated, Lucinda covertly glanced at him while pretending to adjust her bonnet. He looked directly at her, and Lucinda blushed angrily as Major Russell nodded to her as if they were old friends.

"What are those Yankees doing here?" Lucinda heard Mrs. White whisper to Mrs. Hinkle, who shook her head and whispered back, "Spying, no doubt. It they had any real religion, they wouldn't be *here*."

The service began, and although she tried to lose herself in it, Lucinda found it difficult to concentrate on what Pastor Ross said.

Even as she bowed to pray, she felt Major Russell watching her. Was he really there to spy on them? And if so, for what purpose? She decided to ask Major Russell point-blank and see what he had to say for himself.

But when she turned to leave after the benediction, Lucinda saw that the visitors' pew was empty. She sighed, disappointed that the major had escaped before she could confront him.

"This is the smallest Easter congregation in my memory," Mr. Matthews commented as they came out into the sunlight.

"With the Bradleys and the Fletchers both absent, we're lacking a goodly number," said Maurice White, who had overheard the remark.

Did the Bradleys' absence have something to do with Ben? Lucinda wondered.

"That's true," Mr. Matthews agreed, "but they aren't the only ones absent today."

Others joined in the conversation, exchanging stories about their treatment by the federals. Many had been forced to give up their homes or other property and move in with friends or relatives. Some of the missing families with connections in southern Alabama had left town. Several of the men, like Arnold Matthews, had been detained for varying periods. Some had been treated rudely and were highly vocal in their criticism of the harsh martial law that ruled their lives.

"The federals blame the guerrillas for their conduct, but if they continue to mistreat the people of Huntsville, they'll find a whole town full of guerrillas right here," Mr. White declared.

"That's right, boys. We won't stand for it!" exclaimed Bryan Enwood. One of the oldest men in town, he was also among the loudest. Being deaf, he all but shouted when he talked.

"Oh, hush," Bella Enwood said, taking her husband's arm. "I'd best get you home before the Yankees arrest us for inciting to riot."

Although her father chuckled as they walked away from the gossiping group, Lucinda knew that he wasn't amused.

"Talk is cheap," he said in response to her questioning glance. "I'm not worried about what our friends say as much as I am that some of the hotheads might actually heed it. I don't like where that kind of irresponsible talk could lead."

"Do you think some of the men will try to fight the Yankees?"

"Perhaps. As long as we act like civilians, the federals are bound to treat us with some respect. But General Mitchel has made it quite plain that he won't tolerate any sort of resistance. He's even said he'd jail anyone who showed disrespect to a federal soldier. It's a fine line we walk."

"So we must be loyal to our soldiers, but yielding to the rule of the occupation isn't disloyal?"

"It depends on what you mean by yielding. We can honor the enemy's rules without honoring the enemy. But we don't have to *help* them, and I, for one, do not intend to."

They had now come to the McDowell house, where a new flagpole flew the Union and Fourth Ohio flags. Except for a lone sentry at the front door, no one was in sight.

"I wonder what those federals wanted at our church today," Lucinda said as they walked past the house.

"I hope they were getting some religion," her father said. "From all I have seen, many could use it."

"So do I," Lucinda replied. But privately, she doubted

that piety had been the major's motive.

He's up to something, she thought, and wished she knew what.

four

As if to make up for the lovely weather of the previous few days, the heavens opened on Monday and steady rains fell throughout the week. No reply came to General Mitchel in response to his communication to Salmon P. Chase, but on Monday he received a terse message from Secretary of War E. M. Stanton ordering him to report to him daily.

"As if I were some novice lieutenant on his first command!" General Mitchel complained. Seth remained silent, but he hoped that the arrangement might keep him and Buell from continuing their feud. In the meantime, however, Mitchel found it convenient that the rain and high winds would have prevented him from carrying out his orders to destroy the bridges, even if he had wanted to do it.

The next week brought no new crises for the Matthews, although several of the men detained at the same time as Arnold were sent to prison in the North. Lucinda was thankful her father was not in that number, but she could find little else to be grateful for. There was still no word from either Henry or Ben, and the group of young ladies who had gathered to make bandages had disbanded after the wounded soldiers were sent on to northern prisons. Many had since left town with their families. And, for better or worse, she had seen Major Russell only from a distance.

When on Sunday the sun shone brightly, it was a welcome sight. As she dressed for church that morning, Lucinda wondered if Major Russell would be there again. The thought of questioning him gave her something to look forward to, at least.

Suddenly Lucinda heard a commotion in the back of the house. Lige came into the sitting room where Arnold waited for his daughter.

"What is all that racket?" he asked.

"Massa Matthews, Rufe's here—it's about Miz Sherrill."

Lucinda followed her father into the rear hall where Rufe waited, a folded paper in his hand.

"What's happened at Highmeadows?" Arnold asked.

"Miz Sherrill tole me to bring you this, Massa Matthews. Some Yankees on the Pike helt me up, or I'd a'been here sooner."

Mr. Matthews took the paper and read it silently.

"What is it?" Lucinda asked, trying to decipher her father's expression.

"Millie has suffered a double misfortune. Her overseer has left, and she's taken a fall and hurt her ankle."

"How badly?"

"Enough to ask for help. Someone needs to see to it that she can rest until it heals."

"Then I must go to Highmeadows right away," Lucinda said, understanding the situation at once.

Her father walked to the front window and stood for a moment without speaking. The shouts of passing soldiers and the steady tick of the mantel clock were the only sounds in the room until he turned to face Lucinda.

"I wish you didn't have to go, but there's no way I can leave, at least not for the present. I'll try to find an overseer for Highmeadows while you make Millie behave."

Lucinda smiled briefly at the thought of making her strong-willed aunt do anything. "I think I can handle Aunt Millie."

"I'm sure you'll do a better job than I could. And it'll get you out of the constant sight of these federal soldiers."

"When shall I leave?" Lucinda asked.

"As soon as you can get a pass through the picket lines."

"Just to go to Highmeadows?"

"Or anywhere else. That's one of the provisions of the martial law—everyone must have permission to enter or leave the city. That's why Rufe was so frightened. He had a note from Millie saying he was on business for her, as our state law requires, but of course she knew nothing about the other rules."

"I'll have Viola pack some of my things," Lucinda said.

"Yes, and while she's doing that, Lige can see to your horse. Then we'll pay a visit to headquarters."

Lucinda exchanged her Sunday gown for her riding habit, her fingers trembling with excitement as she fastened the tiny buttons on the bodice. She was sorry that Aunt Millie had been hurt, of course, but life at Highmeadows would be a welcome change.

At General Mitchel's headquarters, a guard asked their business and relayed a message through the door, which at length opened to them. Inside, the house looked strange to Lucinda, like a familiar place one sees distorted in a dream. Some of the McDowells' furnishings had been removed to make room for a number of desks and plain chairs, and as they were directed to what had been the McDowells' library, Lucinda wondered what the federals had done with the family's other possessions.

A young lieutenant who obviously enjoyed his power looked up from his desk when Lucinda and her father were ushered into the room.

"Yes?" he asked, his tone suggesting that they were keeping him from important work.

"I am Arnold Matthews and this is my daughter. She requires a pass through the federal lines to be with her injured aunt."

"I have no authority to issue such a pass. If you will come back tomorrow—"

"I need to go today," Lucinda interrupted. "Surely someone here can give me permission."

He's not a day older than Henry, she thought. She knew that he might respond if she smiled and simpered, but that had never been her way, and she certainly didn't intend to start using any feminine wiles on a Yankee, even to get his help.

The lieutenant looked at Lucinda with ill-concealed interest. "Well, maybe I can locate someone," he said.

"That would be appreciated," Arnold said stiffly.

With a nod and another long look at Lucinda, the young officer left the room. They heard voices in the hall, then silence. Lucinda looked around and noted that the room already bore marks of abuse. The carpet was muddied in several spots, and candle wax marred a leather-topped table. Before she could comment on the sad state of affairs, Major Russell entered the room, bowing briefly in their direction.

"Lieutenant Stryker says you have come to request a pass?"

Lucinda lowered her eyes as the major's glance lingered on her, feeling a surge of anger at his boldness. He was a handsome man; there was no question about that. Further, he seemed to be quite aware of the fact and was probably relishing the unsettling effect of his presence on Lucinda.

"My daughter needs to go to her aunt this afternoon," Arnold said. Lucinda looked up to see the major listening impassively to her father's explanation.

"Where is that?"

"Highmeadows Plantation is northeast of Huntsville, due east of the town of Plevna, near Jackson County."

"Show me on this map," the major directed, unrolling a parchment from a stack on the desk.

Lucinda had a glimpse of a detailed map of Madison County, covered with squiggles and strange marks that she could not decipher. Her father traced the route to Highmeadows, pointing to a dot around a group of closely-set lines.

"It's about there," he said.

The major looked at the map a moment longer. "Jackson County is quite a hotbed of guerrilla activity," he commented, then turned to look at Lucinda. "How long will you be there?"

"She may need to stay for several weeks. Is it necessary to know that now?" Arnold answered for her.

The major went to the desk, removed a piece of paper, dipped a quill pen into an inkstand, and began to write. "It is customary, but I'll make this an undated round-trip pass. I trust you won't be traveling alone?" The major spoke to Lucinda, but once more her father replied to his question.

"Mrs. Sherrill's servant Rufe will be with her. I suppose he also needs a pass."

Major Russell looked at Lucinda, half-smiling as if they shared some secret, and she concentrated her gaze on her clenched hands and remained silent.

"Yes. I'll make this an open pass for Miss Matthews and servant to travel between Huntsville and the plantation known as Highmeadows. Your first name, please?"

"Lucinda," Arnold said.

"L-u-c-i-n-d-a?" the major asked, looking to her for confirmation, but she continued to study her hands.

"That's correct," Arnold answered.

Covertly, Lucinda watched the major write, noting that he had a clear hand, legible enough to be read but with enough flourishes to be decorative. Had he always been a soldier? His handwriting suggested he might be a scrivener, perhaps—but of course it was no concern of hers.

The major blotted the paper and handed it directly to Lucinda with a gaze of such intensity that she felt as if he knew exactly what she had been thinking about him.

"I hope your journey will be pleasant," he said, as if the Matthews were social acquaintances, but neither Lucinda nor her father made any reply.

"The major seems civil enough," Mr. Matthews said cautiously when they were safely out of the federal headquarters. "Don't lose that pass. Stay on the main road and show it to the pickets, and you should be all right."

Lucinda nodded but took no comfort in her father's words. In their topsy-turvy new world, she knew that what should happen and what did happen were often opposites. "Viola should have my reticule packed by now," she said.

"I'll have Lige bring Ginger to the front. Come out as soon as you're ready."

Her bag was waiting, so full it threatened to burst its seams.

"Hurry up now," Viola urged. "The daylight's gwine ter

give out afore you git there if'n you don't watch out."

The need for haste made the partings mercifully brief. Clicking to Ginger, Lucinda moved her mount into a fast walk, waved to her father, and left her home behind.

Seth Russell went to a front window and watched Lucinda and her father walk back to their house.

Lucinda, he said softly to himself. The name fit her. *I doubt if anyone dares to call her Cindy.*

Lucinda was so short she had to take two quick little steps to match her father's stride, yet she still managed to look graceful, and her long riding dress only enhanced her shapely figure.

Seth turned away, annoyed with himself for indulging the strange attraction he'd felt since his first sight of Lucinda Matthews. He'd only caught a glimpse of her once or twice in the past week, but seeing her again made Seth realize that his interest hadn't waned.

He also realized that, even with a pass though the Union pickets, the journey Lucinda was undertaking virtually alone was potentially dangerous.

"Private O'Brien!" Seth called to his orderly, who at the moment napped in the former breakfast room.

"Yessir, Major," the youth said, shrugging into his jacket as he came into the hallway. "What is it?"

"I'm going to have lunch now. I'd like to have Star saddled and brought around in about a half hour."

"Will you want me to be going with you?" he asked.

"No, Private, you can have the afternoon off as soon as you've brought my horse. I feel the need to get out of town for awhile."

"Yes, sir!" the boy said, breaking into a grin.

"Where are you going? You'd better be careful, riding about alone," Lieutenant Stryker said when the boy had left the room. "The Rebs would like nothing better than to ambush themselves a real, live Yankee major."

"Thanks for your concern. I'll see you tomorrow."

"But you didn't say where you were going," Lieutenant Stryker called out.

Seth paused at the front door and smiled. "I know," he said, and went out into the mild Sunday sunlight.

Lucinda had known Rufe all her life. He was probably several years older than Lige, with the beginnings of white hair grizzling his head and beard. He had always lived in the country, disliked coming into town, and was glad to get out of it. He was silent as they rode out Meridian Street, past Forestfield Plantation, where the first picket challenged them.

Lucinda showed the pass to a blue-clad soldier, who looking appreciatively at her as he waved them on. Ruefully, she looked down at her dove-gray riding dress, the only garment she owned that allowed her to ride sidesaddle like a lady. With its ruffled bodice and cinched waist, it was more elegant than utilitarian, and Lucinda rarely wore it.

In the Highmeadows pastures she had learned to ride bareback as a child, but when she turned twelve, Aunt Millie had told her she could no longer straddle a horse like a boy. From then on, Lucinda had been made to wear a split skirt and ride sidesaddle, both restrictive to her.

Another picket stopped them near Oaklawn Plantation, where the Robinsons had given one of the gala farewell balls at which she and Ben had danced. Again they were allowed to go on, picking up their pace a bit when they turned onto the Winchester Pike. Lucinda longed to give Ginger her head and gallop in the soft earth beside the road, but Rufe could never keep up on his mule, so she settled for the flat running walk that made Ginger such a delight to ride.

"It's just like sitting in a rocking chair," her father had told her when he brought the little mare back from Tennessee to surprise Lucinda on her sixteenth birthday. The animal's coat was coppery red, so she had been named Ginger. Lucinda had ridden her to Highmeadows more than once, although never in circumstances like the present.

"Tell me how Aunt Millie hurt her foot," Lucinda said after a time.

"I b'lieve she tripped up on a root out by the smokehouse, Miss Lucinda. Her foot had done swole up and turned blue afore we could git her into the house."

"When was that?"

"Three days back, early. It got worser day afore yestiddy, an' that's when she ast me to come fetch help."

"Aunt Millie doesn't give in very easily," Lucinda said, more to herself than to Rufe. "She must be in a lot of pain to ask for help."

"Yes'm, I 'spect she is," Rufe said, and fell silent again.

Lucinda looked around, appreciating the beauty of the day. The ride to Highmeadows was quite scenic, with the newly-green Appalachian Mountains to the east and checkered fields, streams, and woods all around them. Wild roses grew in profusion by the side of the road, and the Flint River was clear and quiet beneath the wooden bridge that spanned it.

They forded several smaller streams before reaching

Plevna, where they rested their animals and ate part of the food that Viola had provided. There were few travelers on the road, but as they approached New Market in the late afternoon, Lucinda could see some activity ahead. Rufe squinted into the distance, then turned to Lucinda, worry lines creasing his forehead.

"Them's Yankees," he said with fear in his voice. "Likely the ones what stopped me afore."

Lucinda patted her pocket, where the pass rustled reassuringly. "They won't bother us now," she said with more assurance than she felt.

A half-dozen mounted soldiers approached them at a canter. A few yards away they halted, and a man with broad sergeant's stripes on his sleeves approached them alone.

"Halt, there! Who are you, and what is your business?"

The man's face seemed unnaturally red, and his voice somewhat thick. A chorus of loud talk and laughter from the rest of the patrol greeted his remarks, and Lucinda quickly concluded that the men had probably been drinking. Silently she handed over the pass.

The sergeant looked at the paper, then at Lucinda and Rufe. His eyes moved to Ginger, and Lucinda felt a faint prickling of apprehension as he swung off his horse and walked around hers.

"Nice little filly you got there. What's a sesech doing with a fine animal like that?"

Lucinda didn't reply, feeling that the less she said, the better.

"Hey, Missy Rebel, I asked you a question!"

The man was close enough for Lucinda to smell the reek of liquor on his breath. In a sudden move he grabbed

Ginger's bridle. Feeling the pressure on her sensitive mouth, the animal tossed her head and shied.

"You're hurting my horse," Lucinda said, more angry than afraid. "Please return my pass and let us go on."

"This is what your pass is worth," the man snarled. Lucinda watched aghast as he tore Major Russell's document into small pieces. "Now, I'll have that horse, mistress. Get down!"

The instant the sergeant dropped Ginger's bridle to pull her from the saddle, Lucinda dug her heels into Ginger's flanks, lowered her head, and lashed the reins against the mare's neck. More surprised than hurt, Ginger bolted, then took off at a full gallop. Lucinda reined her sharply right, away from the road and across an open field. Just past the field was a grove of trees where they might be able to hide.

Lucinda bent low over Ginger's neck and hung on, her right hand knotted in the horses's mane, her left hand clutching the reins and the sidesaddle's horn. As they reached the woods, Lucinda reined Ginger in sharply, lest the horse run under a low-hanging limb and knock her off. Behind her she could hear shouts and pounding hooves and realized that the men were pursuing her.

They might catch me, she thought grimly, *but I won't make it easy for them.*

Lucinda had the double advantage of being sober and knowing the lay of the land. Beyond the woods rose the beginnings of the Appalachian Mountain range that ran north and south to the east, part of the mountain system that rimmed Huntsville. If she made it that far, Lucinda knew she might be able to find one of the numerous limestone caves that dotted the area.

Coming out of the woods, she again spurred Ginger to

a full gallop and again clung fast as a fallen tree loomed ahead. Ginger sailed over it easily, and Lucinda managed to keep her seat, grateful for the horse's fox-hunting experience. She dared not turn to look behind her, but fancied that the shouts were coming from a greater distance than before.

When at last they reached the verge of the mountain, Lucinda slid off and led Ginger into the rock-strewn underbrush. Soon she found a cave opening large enough to conceal them, taking precious moments to persuade Ginger to enter its dark depths.

With trembling legs and a pounding heart, Lucinda sank to the damp ground and waited for her breathing to return to normal. Ginger was lathered and needed to be walked and watered, but Lucinda dared not move from their hiding place. She strained her ears, listening for some evidence that the hunt was still on, but heard only the innocent sounds of a spring afternoon in the woods.

"Well, Ginger. Let's find you some water," Lucinda said at length, patting the horses's velvet muzzle. Ginger nickered softly, almost as if she understood the need for quiet as Lucinda led her out of the cave.

A small stream gurgled nearby, and Lucinda went toward the sound until they came upon the water. Cupping her hand, she bathed her face and slaked her thirst before allowing Ginger to drink.

Lucinda considered the situation and debated whether she should return to the road and look for Rufe. If the soldiers were still there, she would walk right into their hands.

She led Ginger to a spot near the cave and tied her so she could graze in the sparse grass. Then she began to climb the mountain, carefully working her way up to a place where she could look out and see the road. It was slow going as dead underbrush and limbs grabbed at her riding skirt, but despite the scratching and stinging of briars and branches, she kept climbing.

Seeing a flat rock about midway to the top, Lucinda climbed out on it and peered through the screen of greening branches that surrounded her. Yes, there was the stretch of road they had been riding on, and to her right, the grove of trees through which she had ridden on her way to the mountain. The entire scene was devoid of any signs of life. No troops in blue—and no Rufe.

Lucinda sat on the rock, her knees pulled up to her chin, and considered what she should do next. If she went back to the main road, she risked meeting the Union soldiers again, but it was the safest and most direct route to Highmeadows. If she went overland, she would eventually get there, but Ginger was winded, and already the afternoon shadows were lengthening. She had no desire to be traveling after sundown.

Lucinda closed her eyes, praying that she would make the correct choice, and when she opened them again and looked back to the road, she could make out the figure of a man on a mule. Rufe had apparently returned to look for her.

Lucinda scrambled off the rock and back down the hill, sliding and crashing as she went. Her hair had tumbled down around her shoulders and she had lost her hat somewhere, but she hardly noticed.

Leading Ginger to a nearby outcropping of rock, Lucinda remounted and rode back toward the road at a more restful pace. When she broke from the woods, Rufe saw her and waved his hat. As she waved back, a blue-clad figure rode up beside him, and her heart sank. Had she come so far, only to meet the drunken sergeant again?

Never! she resolved. Lucinda turned Ginger sharply and once more rode through the woods. She could hear the horse's labored breathing over her own, and someone shouting behind her. This time her pursuer was very close. Desperately, Lucinda spurred Ginger. She saw the edge of the mountain ahead just as a voice behind her cried out, "Stop! Don't go any farther!"

Lucinda reined Ginger in and sat, breathing raggedly, her eyes downcast. Without looking at the man in blue who had come up beside her, Lucinda spoke. "I will not give up my horse."

"Miss Matthews, are you all right?"

Dazed, Lucinda turned to see not the drunken sergeant she was expecting, but Major Russell. She blinked in surprise.

"Here, let me help you," he said, holding up both hands to assist her to dismount.

Lucinda put her hands on his strong forearms and allowed him to lift her out of the saddle, but as soon as her feet touched the ground, she pulled away and confronted him angrily.

"If I am all right, it's no thanks to your men. Some drunken lout tried to steal my mare."

"I apologize for whatever might have been done. I assure you the men in question will be dealt with. Are you able to ride on?"

As he looked at her with what appeared to be genuine concern, Lucinda was suddenly aware of her unkempt appearance. She glanced at her scratched hands and the wreck of her riding dress and gestured.

"I have to. My aunt expects me before dark. But your sergeant tore up my pass."

"I'm all the pass you need for now. Can your horse be ridden?"

Lucinda glanced at Ginger, contentedly cropping grass and apparently none the worse for their wild ride. "I think she'll be all right if she doesn't have to gallop any more. If you'll just give me another pass, we'll continue our journey."

Major Russell almost smiled. "I'm afraid I didn't bring any writing implements with me, Miss Matthews. But I'll be happy to see that you reach your destination."

"Rufe and I will take our chances," Lucinda said.

"Without a pass, you're likely to be detained by one of our many patrols—unless they think you're guerrillas and shoot you first, of course."

The man is serious, Lucinda thought. Even though she was sure he exaggerated, she realized she had no choice but to accept his escort.

"Then let's go," she said.

Major Russell made a stirrup with his hands and boosted Lucinda into the saddle. As he gave her the reins, his hand lingered a moment on hers with a tingling warmth she felt through her body. Angry that she had both noticed and enjoyed the sensation, Lucinda jerked Ginger's head around sharply and rode away from him. He brought his mount, a large black stallion, beside her and was silent until Lucinda's curiosity made her ask him a question.

"How did you happen to be on this road?"

"It's a nice afternoon for a ride," he replied, smiling at her as if they were old friends. "I'm not on official duty now."

"Maybe those drunken soldiers weren't, either," Lucinda said, determined not to let him forget what had happened to her.

When they reached the road, Rufe looked relieved that Lucinda hadn't been harmed. He didn't seem to trust the major, however, and rode so close behind them that Major Russell asked him to back off.

"My horse is skittish and might kick your mule," he explained, and reluctantly, Rufe obeyed.

"Did Rufe tell you how your soldiers tried to steal my horse?"

"If they did wrong they will be punished," Major Russell said.

"If!" Lucinda exclaimed, her anger freshly rekindled. "The men were drunk, and even if they weren't, they shouldn't have been preying on defenseless civilians."

The major's sudden laugh startled Lucinda. "I'd hardly call you defenseless. You seemed to be handling the matter very well."

"I don't need your compliments, Major!" she exclaimed.

Seeing that she thought he was making fun of her, the major grew more serious. "It's the truth. Not many young ladies would be so brave. And I do realize that living in an occupied town and having to obtain permission to travel can't be very pleasant. You might not believe it, but I can assure you that our role as occupiers is difficult, too."

"It's easy for the conqueror to speak of hardship!" Lucinda exclaimed. "Have you any idea of the damage your troops have already done and will no doubt continue to do?"

"*Some* troops," he corrected. "Do you think things have

gone very differently in northern cities entered by Rebels?"

"I don't know about that, Major Russell. If I had my way, there would never have been a war at all—and certainly no soldiers coming to interrupt our lives."

"Armies exist to fight. They're ill-suited for occupation duty. Sometimes soldiers get restless and misbehave."

"Then I suggest that your army should move on and find soldiers to fight and quit bothering defenseless civilians."

"Nothing would please us more. But you must know that not every civilian in Huntsville is an innocent non-combatant. Some are causing us a great deal of trouble, and as long as that continues, measures must be taken to protect our interests."

"I don't know anyone who's making trouble, but I can name many people who your forces have caused hardship."

"So it appears to you," the major said, then fell silent for a moment. "I wish we could have met under different circumstances. I assure you I have no horns hidden under my hat."

Lucinda resisted the urge to smile at his remark and tried to make her tone severe. "Nor do we, Major. We just want to be left in peace."

"And, incidentally, to keep your slaves and your way of life at the expense of the federal union."

"That is your opinion," she said coolly.

"But surely you must wonder at some of the secessionist views," he went on, pressing the topic. "I saw you at church services. Doesn't the holding of slaves strike you as contrary to religious principles?"

His expression was intent but not unkind, yet Lucinda had no intention of defending a system she had always taken for granted.

"Am I to assume that your presence in church means you are a religious man?"

The major's face registered surprise, then chagrin. "How did my religion get into this conversation?"

"I believe you raised the matter first."

"So I did. Religion apart, I believe that slavery ought to be ended, with or without the sanction of government. It seems to me that anyone who values human life would eventually agree."

"Then you wear the union blue because you're an abolitionist?"

Seth Russell looked directly at her. "No, Miss Matthews. Until the war began, I was willing to live and let live. Unlike the abolitionists, I see many problems in ending slavery all at once."

"Then why did you become a soldier?" Lucinda asked.

"Because I believe that without the South there can be no United States of America. Our people went through too much to gain their independence to let our great potential die because a few men insist on having their own way."

"I've heard the same argument used on the Southern side," Lucinda said. "I doubt that we'd ever agree on its cause, and our arguments certainly won't affect its outcome."

"I agree that we can't change what has already happened, but we can influence the course of the future. Keep that in mind the next time you hear that Rebels have raided our trains. Believe me, it's not in your people's best interest to support such activity."

"As a soldier, you'd fight as long as you had the opportunity. You can't expect less from our men."

"I don't. The sad fact is that we are all alike. I too have a family that cares for me and which I hope to see soon. But for now I have a job to do, just as your brother does."

Lucinda had never thought of the men swarming through Huntsville as having any life other than that involved in making them miserable. That they might have had families and lived in regular houses seemed strange.

What kind of family does he have waiting for him? she wondered. Somehow the major didn't look as if he had a wife and children, but of course Lucinda would never ask any man his marital status.

"What was your job before the war?" she asked instead, assured that he was no professional soldier.

"I practiced law in Cincinnati."

No wonder he's so argumentative, Lucinda thought. She almost said so out loud, but just then they reached a familiar side road.

"Here's the turn, Missy Lucinda," Rufe called out.

"We can go the rest of the way alone," Lucinda said.

"I'll see you safely there," the major said. They ascended the rather steep hill that led to the Highmeadows land in silence. The rapidly deepening twilight lent the forests on either side of the lane an ominous air.

All kinds of things could hide in there, Seth thought. Aloud he said, "I can see how the place got its name."

Then the lane levelled off, and they reached the plateau on which Highmeadows had been built. Behind them was the rising moon, three-quarters full. In the distance behind the house, a higher mountain ridge rose, and just above the horizon was the evening star, shining alone.

Star light, star bright, first star I see tonight, Lucinda thought. As if reading her mind, the major nodded toward the solitary point of light.

"There's Venus to greet you. I suppose you call it a star."

"It is widely known as the Evening Star," Lucinda said.

"But Venus is actually a planet. Planets shine and stars twinkle—that's one way you can tell them apart."

"I am quite aware of that," Lucinda said somewhat stiffly. "I have known the names of all the constellations and planets since childhood."

"That must have been ages ago," the major said in mock seriousness.

"I'm almost nineteen," she said, then quickly regretted it. Her age was certainly none of his business.

"I thought so," he said.

What does that mean? Lucinda wondered, but made no comment as they made the last turn of the lane and the house came into view. Rocks taken from the surrounding hills and cleared from the plateau's meadows formed fences along the front lot and had been used for the double chimneys at each end of the house. Several hounds had begun to bark when they were still far down the lane, so the household was expecting them as they rode up.

Sadie and her oldest daughter, Safira, came out first, followed by Amos, the houseman, who took Lucinda's bag while Rufe led Ginger away to the stable.

"My aunt will want you to come inside and have some food," Lucinda said, telling herself that she owed the major that much courtesy.

"I must be going," he said, looking at the obviously startled servants, who had never seen a Union soldier before.

"Let Rufe feed and water your horse, at least. It's a long ride back to Huntsville."

"Thank you, ma'am, but Star is accustomed to much longer trips," he replied, touching the brim of his hat with his riding crop. "I enjoyed our conversation. Perhaps we'll meet again when you return."

"Perhaps," Lucinda murmured, annoyed that she seemed suddenly tongue-tied. She was determined not to thank him for escorting her and could think of nothing else to say. With a final wave of his hand, the major moved on. Aunt Millie called out to her, and Lucinda turned and entered the house.

Highmeadows was simply built with a central hall that ran its entire length. On either side of the hall were two rooms, with front and rear staircases leading to a second story that was identical to the first.

Normally Aunt Millie occupied the upstairs front bedroom over her parlor, but since her injury, she had stayed downstairs, ensconced on a sofa in the parlor. As her niece entered the room, Millie propped herself on one elbow and slowly swung her feet around to sit up.

With her straw-colored hair streaming down her back and the bright expression in her blue eyes, Millie Sherrill might at first glance pass for Lucinda's older sister. A closer look would reveal the worry-lines in her forehead and the depth of the creases around her ready smile. But there was no doubt that she was pleased to see Lucinda.

"I was hoping you'd come to my rescue," she said, accepting Lucinda's hug. Then, looking more closely at her, "You look awful! Did your horse throw you?"

"No, I'm fine," Lucinda said and related the day's events.

"Where's the Yankee now?" Millie asked when Lucinda finished.

"On his way back to Huntsville, I suppose. I told him you'd want him to have supper before he went back, but he declined."

Millie sighed. "It's just as well that he didn't stay. He wouldn't find a very warm welcome here."

Lucinda drew a chair up to the couch and looked closely at her aunt's injured foot, badly swollen and streaked an angry red. "You ought to be soaking that in hot water and salts. I'll have Sadie bring some in right away."

"But you just got here!" Millie protested. "You need some hot food and a warm bath yourself, from the looks of you. Go along now and have Sadie heat water for us both. When you've eaten and bathed, go on to bed. We can talk in the morning."

"I am tired," Lucinda admitted, feeling her muscles cry out in protest as she stood. "It's good to be back here."

"You're a sight for these sore eyes," Millie said with a broad smile. "If your Papa could see the way you look, he'd just about die."

"Then it's a good thing he can't. I'll see you at break-fast."

After she had eaten and enjoyed the luxury of a warm bath and a rubdown with a fresh linen sheet, Lucinda put on her nightgown and climbed into the old four-poster bed in which she always slept at Highmeadows. Moonlight fell onto the floor beside the bed, making her gown glow white in the darkness and lending a mysterious air of unreality to the familiar room.

Drowsily, Lucinda thought of the major and their conversation. She thought of things she wished she had said and some that she wished she hadn't. She wondered if she would see him again and berated herself for half-wanting to, knowing such desires almost amounted to treason.

Where are you, Ben? Lucinda cried silently, his name a talisman against the night and the strange mood that threatened to engulf her.

Somewhere an owl called in the darkness: her only answer.

five

Seth Russell welcomed the moonlight that washed the road before him. He didn't know this area well, but he was quite aware that he was near intense guerrilla activity. Riding alone, he made a prime target for any marauders who might hear his horse's hoofbeats. Seth moved Star to the far side of the roadway, where the lush spring grass might muffle the sound.

Then, still alert to the conditions around him, Seth settled back in the saddle and allowed himself to think about Lucinda Matthews. He shook his head. He was foolish to waste time thinking of someone who hated all he represented. *She must have a sweetheart,* he thought, *probably a Rebel soldier.*

An owl hooted in the woods and another joined in a few seconds later. "Whoooooo," the first owl called, and the other, "Whoooo-ooo."

"Who, indeed?" Seth said, half-aloud. Not that it mattered, of course. He and Lucinda's Confederate love would never meet.

Suddenly Seth became aware of the sound of a train behind him. Regular trains never ran at night, due to the danger of stray animals wandering onto the track and causing derailments, but General Mitchel had ordered his military trains to make irregular night runs in an attempt to keep the renegade guerrillas from disrupting them.

As the sound of the locomotive grew nearer, Seth turned

his horse into a stand of trees to wait for the train to pass. He had been there only a few moments when he heard a tattoo of hoofbeats on the road he had just left. A half-dozen men rode toward the railroad, and Seth watched helplessly as they placed something on the tracks. If the train's engineer didn't see the obstacle in time, the locomotive might wreck. Seth took his revolver from its holster, ready to ride out and help in case there was a fight.

The locomotive came ever closer, the big wheels grinding and sparking against the rails until, with a terrible squealing of brakes, the huge engine began to shudder to a stop. Seth started from his hiding place, but stopped at the edge of the woods. If he shot his revolver, he might frighten them off—or succeed only in drawing their fire and getting himself killed.

While he debated what to do, Seth saw the guerrillas had boarded and were already leaving the train, some carrying bundles that seemed to be heavy. If they went back the way they came, he would be able to fire at least once. If they scattered, he might be able to capture one of them.

"All right, boys—let's go!" someone shouted, and in another moment the men had remounted and were galloping away, each making for a different point of the compass. One rode directly toward him, his blond hair ghostly in the moonlight. He sat high in the saddle and rode with a rifle in one hand.

Seth turned his horse and spurred him to a gallop when the rider veered off the road and into the woods, trying to calculate the angle at which he could have a clear shot at the man. Firing in the trees was too dangerous; a shot could ricochet and hit him or his horse as easily as its target. The sound of his own horse's hooves would mask that of Seth's mount as long as they stayed in the woods. In the open, it was a different matter.

Seth urged Star out of the trees and across a creek. Just on the other side, the guerrilla rode on, apparently unaware that he was being pursued. Readying his revolver, Seth pulled back the hammer and braced himself for the kick that could knock him from the saddle when he fired. The gun went off, roaring in the night and echoing from the nearby hills, and at the same moment a cloud obscured the moon.

Seth managed to hang on to his seat and pull Star to a halt while he listened in the darkness for any clue to the fate of the man at whom he had fired. At first all was silent, then he heard approaching hoofbeats. He wheeled around as the blond soldier galloped past him, some twenty few yards away. Instinctively Seth bent low over Star's neck, spurring his animal. In a confused blur he heard the man laugh, then the night exploded in a mighty roar as he fired at Seth. The concussion almost knocked him from the saddle, but Seth hung on until Star once again reached the woods.

By then Seth's assailant had disappeared, his horse's hooves a faint echo as he rode east. Seth let his breath out and shook his head. It was the closest he'd come to being killed or injured, and as he rode back toward Huntsville, Seth could scarcely believe that only a few minutes before he had been seriously thinking of a Rebel girl.

That sort of thing has to stop, he told himself. His life could depend on it.

The day began early at Highmeadows, but Lucinda slept deeply, unaware of the early morning chatter of the birds or the imperious crowing from the barnyard. She opened her eyes to the familiar flowered wallpaper, then winced when she tried to stretch herself awake. She ached all over as she dressed and crept down the stairs. Millie laughed when she saw her.

"You look like nursing me, young lady, when you can hardly walk yourself! Maybe I can find a sofa for you, too."

"I'm just a little stiff," Lucinda replied from the doorway. She tried to stand straight, but stopped as pain shot through her back.

"Get some food inside you. Then come back and we'll talk."

Lucinda went into the dining room, where the windows overlooked a velvety green pasture that merged with the lighter spring-green of the mountain behind it. Wisps of fog lingered on the hilltops, but the bright sun promised a fair day.

Gratefully, Lucinda accepted the fried ham and red eye gravy, beaten biscuits, and molasses served up by Safira. Except for the coffee, everything had come from Highmeadows, and by the time Lucinda returned to Millie, she felt much better.

"How is your foot this morning?" Lucinda asked, and Millie raised it for inspection.

"The heat seems to help. I had another long soak this morning. Now sit down and tell me what's happening in town."

Briefly, Lucinda sketched what she thought would interest her aunt. "One of the worst things is not knowing what's going on in the outside world," she finished. "According to the Yankees, we haven't won a single battle since they arrived."

"And Henry? Any word of your brother?"

Lucinda shook her head. "They were at Yorktown the last we heard. We'd hoped they would be furloughed, but of course they can't come home."

"What else is going on?" Millie asked.

"There are a lot of guerrillas operating around Huntsville and making General Mitchel very unhappy."

"No doubt," Millie said dryly. "Well, it's a bad business all around, and to top it all, here I am, helpless as a babe, having to depend on a slip of a girl to keep Highmeadows going."

Although the words were spoken with a smile, Lucinda felt her aunt's frustration. "I'm ready—just tell me what must be done."

"Among other things, the cotton needs chopping and the late garden must be planted. Since Mr. Cameron left, I fear that the hands have slacked off."

"Where did your overseer go?"

"He *said* he was joining a Confederate unit, but I have my doubts. At least he waited until we had the cotton planted."

"You should have told Papa. He could have found someone for you before now."

"Until this accursed fall, I was doing the job very well myself, thank you," Millie said, waving her hand at her injured foot. "All I want is to hang on until Henry comes back and takes over the place. Then I'll come to town like everyone keeps telling me I should and find myself a shady veranda and a rocking chair."

The image of her energetic aunt rocking her days away was so ludicrous that Lucinda smiled. "I'll believe that when I see it. But for now, you'd better put me to work."

An hour later, armed with several pages of notes she'd

made as Millie talked, Lucinda sat down at Buck Sherrill's desk and opened the heavy black ledger that contained the transactions and expenses of the day-to-day operations of Highmeadows. Although it was a small plantation compared to many in Madison County, it was still a complex, almost self-contained world. As with any society, its smooth functioning depended on the working together of a number of people.

All told, Highmeadows was home to more than forty slaves, for whose welfare Millie Sherrill was completely responsible. With the departure of the overseer, who had dealt with the yard and field hands, every detail of running the place had been left to Millie. It was a daunting job, even for an able-bodied man.

No wonder Aunt Millie asked for help, Lucinda thought as she looked over the list of hands the Sherrills owned. Rufe was the most trusted servant. Although officially he was in charge of the livestock, he also picked up supplies, took corn and wheat to be milled, and delivered messages. His wife, Sadie, served as the housekeeper, and their daughter Safira cooked for Millie and the household staff.

Amos, the houseman, was a mute who understood what was said to him. His wife, Rhoda, did most of the housecleaning and laundry. In addition to the house servants, there were yard hands in charge of the poultry and the flower and vegetable gardens. The largest group, the field hands, did the physical labor of plowing, hoeing, weeding, cultivating, and harvesting the crops. At critical times in the cotton-growing cycle, everyone worked in the fields.

Lucinda knew all the house and yard hands and most of the field workers from her long childhood summers there. For a moment she closed her eyes, remembering the days when she and Henry had roamed the farm at will, from the top of the mountain behind the house to the creek bottom at the foot of the Highmeadows plateau. They had ridden on hay wagons and straddled plow mules as they plodded over the fields. They had played hide-and-seek in the hay barn, where dust motes danced in the light filtering in through the boards. They had picked blackberries and sucked nectar from honeysuckle and pretended that Henry already owned this land which he had always known would someday be his.

Lucinda sighed and opened her eyes. How devoutly she wished that Henry were here in her place! But he wasn't, and she had work to do.

Over lunch, eaten from trays in the parlor so Millie wouldn't have to leave the sofa, Lucinda told her aunt she had gone over the accounts and understood what needed to be done to insure Highmeadows' survival.

"You're off to a good start," Millie said when Lucinda finished her report, "but right now my main concern is making a cotton crop. Without the cash from it...," Millie stopped, unwilling to pursue the thought.

"Don't worry. God will take care of us. I'm sure we'll manage just fine."

"Ah, Lucinda, you're a life-saver," Millie said with a fond smile. "To be young and optimistic and have such faith must be wonderful. Did I give you the planting schedule?"

"Have you heard the news, sir?"

Lieutenant Stryker stuck his head into the doorway, startling Seth so that he nicked himself with his straight razor.

"You could at least knock," he said, putting down the razor and pressing a towel to his cheek.

"Sorry. But did you hear about the latest guerrilla raid?"

"No. I came in very late last night and I just got up."

"Well, about thirty guerrillas stopped a train heading here and stole some gold and supplies. What do you think about that?"

"Thirty guerrillas, you say?" Seth asked, knowing he had counted six.

"At least! We ought to go out in force and wipe them out."

"Do you know where to find them, Lieutenant?" Seth asked. He stropped his razor and tested its edge before continuing to shave.

"No, of course not. But—"

"Have you been outside the city since we came here?" Seth asked.

"Well, no, I haven't," Stryker admitted, looking puzzled.

"Then I suggest that you leave the strategy of dealing with the guerrillas to your senior officers. Close the door behind you," he added, although the young lieutenant had made no sign of leaving.

"Yes, sir. But you might tell the general what I said."

The door closed a fraction of a second before Seth's soap hit it. Feeling somewhat better after venting his anger, Seth retrieved the rough, homemade bar he had found in the Allison store room and finished shaving. He knew he shouldn't let Lieutenant Stryker bother him, but he was on edge from lack of sleep. He would give the general his version of the events of the past evening, even though explaining how he happened to witness them could be awkward.

But Stryker was right about one thing: something had to be done about the guerrillas, and soon.

Lucinda was relieved that she had no trouble convincing the hands that the little slip of a girl who had to stand tiptoe to see over her horse when she mounted was now giving them orders. Most took the change well, with only a few seeming to resent her presence.

After she'd made sure that the large garden that had to feed them all was being properly cared for, Lucinda turned her attention to cotton, the only big cash crop. After she had been at Highmeadows for a few days, Lucinda sought out Turk, the slave who had been given charge of the field hands, and asked him to see that the planting was carried out as soon as possible.

She had just left him when a commotion erupted in the vicinity of the hog lot, and Lucinda went to investigate. She found Nancy, the slave who slopped the hogs, spanking a little boy. Upset by the child's piercing screams, the hogs thrashed around wildly and squealed as if they were being fatally stuck.

"What are you doing to that child?" Lucinda cried. The woman looked up but continued to strike the boy she held by the scruff of his neck.

"This no-good young'un done let two hogs get out," she said.

"Please let the boy go. Whatever he's done, beating him half to death can't undo it."

Nancy dropped the stick and pushed the boy away. "He needs a lesson," she said sullenly. "When hog-killing time comes and meat's short, I'se the one that'll git the blame."

Suddenly aware of the smelly mire in which they stood, Lucinda wrinkled her nose and backed away from the pigs, glancing around the lot as she did so. "Is there a hole in the fence? Or maybe the hogs could have rooted their way out?"

"No'm," Nancy replied firmly, her anger now evaporated. "They ain't no holes in the fence, and the pigs cain't root with them rings in they snouts."

"Then what could have happened to them?"

Nancy looked darkly at the boy, whose sobs had subsided to soft hiccoughs. "That worthless young'un is sposed to watch the pigsty of a night, but I finds him here this mornin' sound asleep, and two o' the best shoats gone."

"Who would take them?" Lucinda asked, but Nancy only shrugged.

"Perhaps the boy is too small for that kind of work," Lucinda suggested. "I'll speak to Mrs. Sherrill immediately and see if we can spare someone older to watch the hogs."

Nancy mumbled something that could have been assent, and with a final glance at the boy, Lucinda left the hog lot and cut across a fallow field to the barn. The cows had been let out to graze, and Ginger whinnied to her from the adjacent paddock. Lucinda wished she could take her for a pleasant ride, but there was too much to be done to spare the time just now.

Lucinda entered the barn, where Buck Sherrill's stallion, Midnight, pawed and snorted in his stall. A powerful, dangerous horse, he was kept stabled when Ginger was in the paddock.

Near the door, Rufe was shoveling out other stalls and preparing to put down fresh straw. Seeing Lucinda, he stopped and leaned the pitchfork against the stall door.

"Rufe, I just learned that a couple of hogs are missing. Do you know anything about it?"

"No'm, I shore doesn't."

"Has anything else been missed that you know about?"

Rufe pursed his lips and scratched his head. "Well'm, Betty did 'low as how her hens ain't layin' lak they should, an' thought mebbe somepun wuz takin' eggs from the nestes, but that's all."

He knows more than he's telling me, Lucinda thought, but of course there was nothing she could do about it. Thanking him, she turned back toward the house, puzzling about what she should do. Petty thievery was hardly a serious matter, but if the losses continued, the food supply at Highmeadows would be in danger. In the summer kitchen, Safira told her that some staples had lately disappeared, and Lucinda went in to report the losses to Millie.

"Has anything like this ever happened before?" she asked as she concluded her report.

Millie shrugged, not seeming to be very disturbed by her niece's news. "On a place like this we can't lock up everything. Sometimes we have to look the other way and let the slaves think they're getting by with something. I suppose it keeps them happy, after a fashion."

Just then the dogs set up a racket, and they heard the sound of rapidly approaching horses coming up the path to the house. Lucinda ran to the front door and was confronted by a half-dozen federal soldiers. At first she feared it was the patrol she had crossed on her way to Highmeadows, but then she saw Major Russell and felt a surge of relief.

"Pardon me, Miss Matthews," he said, touching the brim of his hat. "We're looking for a band of guerrillas that might be in this area."

"Guerrillas around here?" Lucinda questioned, as if the idea were totally ridiculous. "I'm not aware of any."

"Nevertheless, we must look. Please stay inside until we leave."

His tone was not unpleasant, but he obviously meant business. Lucinda did as she was told, watching from window to window as the men spread out around the house, poking and prodding as they went. Two soldiers entered the house, their footsteps sounding loudly as they passed from room to room. They peered under the furniture and poked behind the curtains, reminding Lucinda of the first time she had seen Major Russell.

A few minutes later Seth came into the parlor, and somewhat awkwardly, Lucinda introduced him to her aunt.

"So you're the Yankee who brought Lucinda here," she said.

"Yes, I am, Mrs. Sherrill. I hope you haven't been bothered by any of our men since then," he said politely, his face a study of concern.

Oh, he's a charmer, Lucinda thought as she watched the sudden color that came into her aunt's face. *I'm not the only one who sees that Seth Russell is an attractive man.*

"No, and I hope we never do. We're just two lone women here, and we certainly know nothing about any guerrillas."

"Of course, ma'am," Seth said. "Miss Matthews, you'll be glad to know that we found the patrol that accosted you, and all the men have been disciplined."

"I don't suppose you hanged them, did you, Major?" Lucinda asked.

Seth Russell's pleasant expression never wavered. "Not quite, but the sergeant will be a private when he gets out of the stockade. I don't think he'll ever bother another civilian."

"I should hope not! But that reminds me, Major. When I'm ready to return to Huntsville, I'll need a pass. Will you give me another one?"

"Certainly, Miss Matthews. Now about the guerrillas—"

"I told you, we know nothing about any guerrillas," Millie interrupted, and Lucinda was surprised at the edge in her aunt's voice.

"For your sake, I hope it stays that way. They have a way of taking what they want without asking any questions."

"Just like the Yankees, you mean?" Lucinda said, unable to resist the comment.

"You're through here, Major?" Millie said before he could reply.

Seth nodded, once more adopting the expressionless mask that he had worn the first time Lucinda had seen him. "Quite. We have several other places to visit, so I'll bid you good day, Mrs. Sherrill." He half-bowed in Lucinda's direction. "Miss Matthews."

"I'll see you out," Lucinda said, ignoring Millie's frown.

"I'll tell your father that you and your aunt are all right," Seth said when they reached the front veranda.

"Have you seen Papa recently? Is he well?" she asked.

"Yes, on both counts. Mr. Matthews has been quite useful to us as a liaison between our staff and Huntsvillians."

"Oh," Lucinda said. She had been looking into his eyes

as he spoke, and suddenly she felt that she was drowning in their dark depths. He stood close to her but made no move to touch her, although she sensed that he would like to. *And I wouldn't mind if he did,* she thought, both surprised and angry at herself for wondering, even briefly, how his arms would feel around her.

Aware that his men were waiting for him and listening to their conversation with interest, Seth touched his hat again. "Goodbye," he said, and untied his horse from the hitching post just beyond the house.

As suddenly as they had come, the men left, apparently without having caused any damage or taken anything away. Lucinda watched the cloud of red dust that marked the riders' progress down the hill, then went back into the parlor.

"That major is a dangerous man," Millie greeted her.

"Dangerous? They didn't do any damage," Lucinda replied.

"That's not what I mean, Lucinda—I saw the way he looked at you."

"I think you must be mistaken," Lucinda replied. "I wonder why he thought there are guerrillas here?"

"I have no idea, but those men saw our valuables. I've been thinking that we ought to round up some of the best things and hide them, in case the next bunch isn't so polite."

"That's probably a good idea," Lucinda agreed, and after some discussion the two women decided that they would allow Amos, and Amos alone, to help them.

Choosing and packing valuables took the rest of that day. Millie settled for removing only the best silverware, a Chinese vase Buck had given her as a wedding gift, some gold coins, and her best jewelry. After some thought, they decided to bury the things in Midnight's stall.

"That horse might turn out to be of some use to you yet," Lucinda said with a smile. No one but Buck had ever dared to ride him, and although Millie sometimes spoke of selling him, she had never had the heart to part with her husband's mount.

"Tell Rufe to leave Midnight in the paddock tonight," Millie directed. "You and Amos can hide the things after midnight."

That night, Lucinda went upstairs and pretended to go to bed, but instead she wrote a letter to Henry, hoping that Major Russell might be able to get the letter safely away if she asked him to mail it for her.

He didn't give me a pass back to Huntsville, she suddenly realized. Not that it mattered, since she had no idea how much longer she would have to stay at Highmeadows. Perhaps she should write him and ask him for a new pass, anyway. Surely that much contact with the enemy would do no harm.

Lucinda waited until the mantel clock in the parlor chimed twelve times before creeping down the front stairs. As arranged, Amos was waiting for her, and they began moving the valuables, wrapped in sheeting and old quilts, to the barn. The waning moon provided the only light, but once everything was inside the barn, Amos lit a small lantern and began to dig in the muck of Midnight's stall.

As the hole was made ready, Lucinda stood watch, then helped Amos lower the bundles into it. Had they a coffin, she reflected, it would be about the right size to hold the treasured items. But the cloth would suffice, at least for the immediate future.

Lucinda shivered as Amos replaced the dirt, carefully tamped it down, and threw fresh straw on top. A cool night breeze had sprung up, and clouds covered the moon as they left the barn.

Amos went toward his quarters, and Lucinda had her hand on the barnyard gate when she heard the distant sound of barking dogs. The Highmeadows hounds ran free, and at night they often roamed the countryside, treeing 'coons and pursuing rabbits, so their noise wasn't unusual. But there was something else, something not quite right.

Lucinda turned back toward the barn and stood against the boards, straining to see into the darkness. She could make out nothing, but the dogs seemed to be getting closer. Then they fell unaccountably silent. An owl hooted, and somewhere a twig snapped.

Lucinda held her breath as the moon came from behind the clouds to reveal three figures emerging from the woods. They crept toward the smokehouse, which stood between the barn and the hog lot. At first Lucinda was sure they must be Yankees, come back to steal where they had earlier searched. But then she realized that these intruders wore light-colored clothing—white shirts, surely, and what looked like Confederate gray trousers.

One man entered the smokehouse and emerged a moment later, carrying something on his shoulder. Another of the group went to the henhouse, his progress marked by a series of squawks from its roosting occupants. Lucinda pressed closer to the barn and hoped that they'd come close enough for her to confirm their identity, but they never did.

The silent tableau continued as the men visited several of the outbuildings before leaving the way they had come, melting back into the woods. Lucinda began to run in the direction the men had taken, but as soon as she reached the pitch blackness at the edge of the woods, she realized the folly of her action and stopped.

Although the reason for their presence seemed obvious, she didn't know for certain what side they were on. If they *were* Confederates, why had they sneaked in by night instead of just riding up to the front door in broad daylight and asking for help? Certainly Aunt Millie would gladly give them anything they needed. And if they *weren't* Confederates, who were they?

Seth Russell bent over a series of area maps, examining the spots where guerrillas had been seen in operation.

"This area looks suspicious, Major," Captain Warren said, jabbing at the map in the vicinity where Seth had seen the guerrillas in action himself. "I'd wager their headquarters are somewhere east of there."

"But where? Those mountains hide a lot of secrets, Captain."

"Well, we've scouted all the plantations thereabouts and found nothing. We can't spare the manpower to search more than a small area at a time, and in the meantime, these guerrillas are running wild."

"It would be hard for a guerrilla force of any size to operate very long without being detected," Seth said. "We'll find them."

After the Captain left, Seth walked to the front parlor of the federal headquarters and looked down the street at Lucinda's house. He continued to think of her—probably much too often for his own good. When he realized he'd left Highmeadows without giving her another pass, he had taken one to Arnold Matthews, who said he had no idea when she would be able to use it.

I hope she comes back soon, Seth thought, knowing that if she didn't, he'd have to find a reason to make another trip to Highmeadows.

Seth turned away from the window with a sigh. First, he had to deal with the guerrillas.

six

The next morning, Sadie served breakfast with the news that Rufe had seen rain signs in the moon the night before, and for a moment Lucinda wondered if Rufe had witnessed the midnight burial in the barn or the ensuing events.

After she finished eating, Lucinda went to ask Rufe to take her letters to Huntsville. He was in the barn grooming Midnight, and if he had noticed anything different about the condition of the stall, he said nothing about it.

"I have some letters I'd like you to take to Mr. Matthews, but Sadie tells me you think we're in for rain," she said. "Could you go this morning?"

"Yes'm, I reckons so," Rufe replied, putting down the curry comb. "If I gets started now, I might could beat it."

"Get ready and come on to the house, then. Mrs. Sherrill will want to see you before you go."

Millie wrote a note to Arnold and handed it to Rufe. "If the weather turns bad, stay in town," she said.

When he left, Lucinda turned to her aunt. "Do you trust Rufe?

"With my life. Why do you ask?"

Lucinda hesitated, unsure if she should tell her aunt what she'd seen the night before. "Oh, I don't know. I guess I'm just suspicious of everyone these days."

Millie leaned back against the sofa and sighed, her gaze steady. "These are strange times, Lucinda. Sometimes we have to trust others, even when we don't understand why they may do certain things. Will you remember that?"

Not clearly comprehending her aunt's meaning but aware that Millie had said all she intended to for the time being, Lucinda nodded.

On Monday morning, Lucinda awoke early, as she had become accustomed to doing, and was surprised to see that Millie was already up.

"I'm going out to the fields today," Lucinda said as they had breakfast. "The cotton chopping should be done before the rain starts."

"Yes, that's true. Maybe by the next chopping, I'll have a regular overseer to see to it."

"For your sake, I hope so. I'm riding Ginger today so I can cover more ground."

"Very well, but be careful and stay close in," Millie warned. "You never know what might be out in the woods, and if anything should happen to you, your papa would never forgive me."

"I'm not going into the woods," Lucinda reminded her aunt. She put on her riding dress, glad that Safira had removed the ruffles and made it much more serviceable.

The hands were already working when Lucinda started her rounds. Aware of the need to complete the task, all but the very oldest and the babies were in the fields. Lucinda complimented Turk on the efficient way the work was being done under his direction. After she had made a circuit of the cotton fields, separated because of the terrain, she was satisfied that the work was going well.

The sky was still an even gray but not immediately threatening. It was just past midmorning, and Lucinda didn't want to go back to the house just yet. Finding herself in the most distant field, she decided to ride into the back meadow, always one of her favorite places.

At Lucinda's urging, Ginger broke into a jolting trot, then settled into a canter as Lucinda lightly used her whip. At the end of the cultivated land Lucinda slowed the mare to a comfortable flat running walk and guided her along the wavering trail that cattle had made to the back pasture. The open meadow gave way again to a hardwood thicket, then to a small open area. To the rear of the clearing stood a very old log cabin, a place dear in Lucinda's childhood memories.

Lucinda dropped the reins and slid to the ground, loosely tying Ginger to a sapling at the edge of the woods. Once she had spent hours playing in this cabin, and as she walked toward it she thought how long ago those days seemed. Avoiding some rotten boards in the porch, Lucinda pushed open the door and went inside.

The cabin had always been dark, even on the sunniest days. On this cloudy day, the interior was extremely dim. Yet even in the gloom, Lucinda saw that the cabin was occupied. Several quilts were scattered about, along with wooden boxes that contained various kinds of food. As her eyes adjusted to the dimness, she saw the glint of metal in a corner—a rifle topped by a bayonet.

At once Lucinda realized that soldiers must be using the cabin and that she must leave before they found her there. She turned, only to run headlong into a man who had silently come up behind her.

"Welcome, Miss Lucinda," a familiar voice said, and Lucinda swayed as if she had been physically hit. She'd never fainted, but she was sure she must be close to it as she raised her eyes and saw the speaker. He was tall, blond, and bearded, and he broke into a slow, full-lipped smile as he waited for Lucinda to recover enough to speak.

"Ben!" she exclaimed, but it came out almost as a whisper. "What are you doing here?"

"I could ask you the same thing," he said. "But first, you might look a little happier to see me."

"I'm too surprised," Lucinda said, looking at him more closely.

If anything, Ben Bradley was taller. He was definitely thinner; his full beard needed a trim; and his hair had obviously not been cut in some time. Lucinda had often imagined meeting Ben again when he would come home to Huntsville, triumphant in victory and wearing his gray uniform like a young prince. This meeting certainly bore no resemblance to her daydreams, any more than Ben himself looked as she had thought he would. In sharp contrast to the elegant dress uniform he'd worn at their parting, his plain gray trousers and once-white shirt were dirty and torn in several places.

"I'd have been surprised to see you, but I saw your horse first."

"What are you doing out here by yourself?"

"One thing at a time. Here, let's sit down," he suggested, closing the door and motioning toward the quilt pallet.

"That looks like Aunt Millie's," Lucinda remarked as Ben folded another patchwork quilt into a cushion for her.

"It is. There, that should be more comfortable."

"And the hams and eggs and things—I suppose you took them too?"

Ben sat down across from Lucinda and nodded. "Yes, we took them."

"We? Who else is here?" she asked, recalling the trio in

the barn lot.

"A couple of men you don't know, cut off as I was from their outfits."

"Did you try to come home on a furlough?"

"Not exactly. There was a big fight up in Tennessee before the Yankees took Huntsville—I guess you heard about that?"

Lucinda nodded, and he continued. "Well, after it was over I got a scouting assignment in the area and found out that the federals had taken Huntsville. I met some other fellows and we decided to stay here for a while and see what we could do."

"But how did you happen to come to Highmeadows? And why didn't you let Aunt Millie know you were on the place? She's hurt her ankle and I came to help her—"

"So that's why we haven't seen her lately," Ben put in. "I wondered where she was."

"Do you mean that Aunt Millie knows you're here?" Lucinda asked, finding it hard to believe when Ben nodded.

"I remembered being here with Henry when we were boys, and I hoped your aunt would let us stay on the place. We came in late one night and she met us on the veranda with a shotgun. When she saw that we weren't Yankees, she gave us some food and bedding and told us we could use this cabin. We haven't seen her since."

Lucinda recalled her aunt's dismissal of her reports of the petty thievery on the place and realized that it fit with what Ben was saying.

"I don't understand why she didn't let me know you were here."

"I'm sure she thought it was for the best. Now, tell me

about what's happening in town, how the people feel—everything."

"That's a large order," Lucinda said. "Of course I haven't been there lately myself, but your family was fine the last time I saw them."

Ben nodded as if he already knew that. "Go on. What is the occupation like?"

Lucinda told him what she had shared with Aunt Millie, including her father's detention but omitting any mention of Major Russell.

"What sort of man is this General Mitchel?" Ben asked.

"He's a hard man, I think, all too ready to punish the whole town for the acts of others."

"How do you mean?" Ben asked, and Lucinda told him about the guerrillas' raids and the threatened retaliation for them.

Ben was silent, appearing to ponder her words. In the quiet they became aware that rain had begun to beat a steady tattoo on the tin roof, softly at first, then with more force. Lucinda rose to her feet.

"I was hoping the hands could get the cotton chopped before the rain started," she said, peering anxiously out the window.

Ben seemed amused. "Somehow I can't imagine you playing at overseer," he said.

"I'm not playing," Lucinda replied, stung by his tone. "Someone has to do it, although I hope to be replaced very soon."

"I sent you a letter by Ollice Kinnard. Did he give it to you?"

Years ago, Lucinda thought, *when I was someone else altogether.* She nodded her head.

"Lucinda, I can't tell you what it means to see you," Ben said, gazing into her eyes with the same intense expression she had seen at their parting.

"It's good to see you, as well. When I heard about the battle at Shiloh Church, I prayed you were all right."

Her words reflected her concern, but the emotions she had expected to experience at this meeting weren't there. Sensing her mood, Ben didn't move to take her into his arms, although it was obvious that he wanted to.

"I needed your prayers, believe me. War isn't at all what I thought it would be," he said instead. "I've seen and done things—"

"I have to go now," Lucinda murmured, turning toward the door. She didn't want to hear Ben's war experiences—she already knew they must have been terrible.

"Don't leave yet. You'll just get soaked. At least wait until the rain slacks up."

"That might be a long time. Rufe said we could be in for several days of rain, and he's usually right."

"But he went off this morning anyway, didn't he?"

"How did you know that?" Lucinda asked, uneasy at the thought that Ben and his companions had been spying on them.

"I just know," he said. "When will you be back?" he added as she put her hand on the door, determined to leave.

Lucinda looked at Ben, her thoughts in tangled confusion. This was obviously the same Ben Bradley she'd known all her life, yet something about him had changed in a way that she didn't understand. His question and her answer to it seemed to be important to them both.

"Is there anything you need?" she asked, countering with her own question.

"We can always use food."

"I'll see that you get some, then. Where are your friends, by the way? You said there were three of you."

"Away. We have two horses for the three of us, so we take turns staying here, as a rule. Oh, Miss Lucinda—"

Ben moved toward Lucinda and she did not resist when he gently gathered her in his arms. His lips moved against her forehead, and his beard felt unexpectedly silky against her cheek. Then he groaned and shook his head as he let her go.

"You've lost weight," was all Lucinda could think to say, and he smiled ruefully.

"So I have."

Ben walked outside with Lucinda and gave her a boost up into the saddle. Then he quickly stepped back as if afraid to stay too close. "I hope to see you again very soon," he said formally, as he might to a customer in a cotton deal.

"Goodbye, Ben. Be careful."

He stood in the rain and watched her ride away, waving when she turned for one last look before she left the clearing. He seemed so forlorn that for a moment she was tempted to go back and try to comfort him. But instinctively, Lucinda knew it would be wrong for both of them, and she rode on, scarcely aware of the steady rain. By the time she returned to the house, Lucinda was thoroughly soaked.

"I was beginning to be concerned about you," Millie said when her bedraggled niece entered the parlor. "Turk came in an hour ago and said they'd finished just as the rain came. I asked him if he'd seen you and he said you'd ridden off somewhere. That's quite unwise, you know—and you should get out of those wet clothes."

"I will change them presently, but first we must talk."

"About what?" Millie asked.

"I know about the soldiers in the old cabin. I met one of them this morning, and he told me you knew they were staying here."

Lucinda paused to give Millie the opportunity to speak, but her aunt remained silent, her lips pursed in a way that indicated her distaste for the subject.

"Why didn't you tell me? You must know they've been taking things, yet you let me believe that the hands were probably to blame. I'd like to know what else is going on."

Millie sighed and cocked her head to one side, as if appraising her niece. "In a way, so would I. The boys came by a few days before I fell and asked if they could stay here for a while. The only one I knew was Ben Bradley, and at first I didn't even recognize him, it'd been so long since I'd seen him. They said they didn't intend to cause any trouble and promised to keep out of sight.

"I presumed they would move on in a day or two. Then I had my accident." Millie looked at her foot, still stiff and swollen, and grimaced. "I couldn't get around to check up on them. When you told me about the missing things, I couldn't be certain they had taken them."

"But you should have told me they were here," Lucinda insisted. "I should've known something that important."

Millie half-smiled at Lucinda's indignation. "Child, you have no business knowing about some things. If I'd thought it would serve any purpose, I would have told you."

Lucinda deliberately ignored being called a child—as hard as she had been working, she knew she deserved better—and tried to stifle her anger. "In any case, something needs to be done with them. It would be more sensible to take stores to them than to risk having the hands see them when they prowl around at night."

"That's true," Millie admitted, "but I really thought they'd be gone by now. Surely they must have somewhere else to go."

"I'll take some food to them and find out their plans. I suppose I could go back today," Lucinda said, peering out at the dreary landscape.

"No, that would be foolish. There's no need to get soaked twice in one day. Wait until tomorrow morning."

Lucinda nodded. "All right. And I hope you're not hiding any other secrets!"

By nightfall, with the rain continuing its steady fall, Lucinda and Millie realized that Rufe had probably taken their advice and stayed in town. Soon after the evening meal, Lucinda settled her aunt on the sofa and went up to her room, her mood as dreary as the weather.

Seeing Ben should have given her something to look forward to, but it had had the opposite effect. Lucinda lay on her bed and closed her eyes, trying to recapture her feelings for Ben those long months ago when he left with the band playing and flags flying. For months, she had worried over his safety and longed to see him. But now she had, and it was nothing like she'd thought it would be. When she saw him again, would she feel any differently?

The next morning, the whole world was a uniform dull gray. The rain had stopped, and fog rose from the earth to meet the clouds brooding atop the mountains. No one was stirring when Lucinda slipped away from the house carrying a rucksack of provisions and some shirts she'd found in Henry's room. She walked far to the south of the quarters to make certain that she wouldn't be seen. Except for the final patch of woods on the down side of a steep hill, the way wasn't hard, and within fifteen minutes Lucinda had arrived at the clearing.

She rested her sack on the porch and rapped lightly on the sagging cabin door. At first there was no response, and Lucinda had almost decided that the soldiers had gone when the door opened a cautious crack.

"Who goes there?" a hoarse voice demanded. Before Lucinda could reply, she heard Ben.

"It's Miss Matthews. Let her in, quickly."

Lucinda stepped into the gloom of the cabin and almost onto a sleeping figure who grunted and awoke, rubbing his eyes as if Lucinda had appeared from a particularly wonderful dream.

"This is Thomas," Ben said, nodding toward the swarthy young man who had opened the door, "and Sleeping Beauty here is Leon."

Lucinda acknowledged the introductions as gracefully as she could and tried to ignore the curious stares of Ben's companions.

"What brings you out so early in this miserable weather?" Ben asked when he had retrieved the rucksack and closed the door.

"Aunt Millie asked me to bring you some food and find out how much longer you plan to stay."

"Come back here," Ben invited, taking her elbow and steering her away from the others. A partition marked the far corner of the cabin, and Ben and Lucinda sat down behind it. She watched Ben inspect the contents of the rucksack. "Have you had breakfast?" he asked.

"No, but this is for you. I'll eat when I get back. And I

can bring you more food tomorrow, if you're still here."

Ben smiled and put down the sack. "Why do I get the idea that we're not very welcome?"

"It's not that, but you must know you're in great danger as long as you're in this area. Why, a Yankee patrol was here just a few days ago, looking for guerrillas. If they'd found you all—"

"We know what would happen," Ben said soberly. "But before we try to return to our lines, I want to take back some information."

"What kind of information?"

"Anything we can find out about the federals in Huntsville will help us get them out of there. How many troops there are, where the chief defenses are located, things like that."

"How can you possibly get that kind of information? You don't dare show your faces anywhere near town. There are pickets and patrols everywhere."

"That's quite true," he agreed. "I'd thought we could sneak in at night, until we had to outrun a patrol. Someone else will have to be our eyes and ears—someone who can pass freely in and out of town without suspicion."

"Do you have anyone in mind?" Lucinda asked, already knowing from the intent way Ben was regarding her what he would say.

"I do. Someone who is brave and resourceful and. . .," Ben paused and took one of Lucinda's hands in his. "Someone who means a great deal to me. Will you help us, Lucinda?"

His tone and the touch of his hand echoed the emotions that Lucinda had experienced when she and Ben had said goodbye, and for a brief instant she almost recaptured that feeling. Then it was gone, and it seemed wrong for her to allow Ben to hold her hand and speak of feelings she didn't share. Lucinda gently disengaged her hand.

"What would you want me to do?"

Ben smiled and looked as if he would like to hug her, but did not. "Walk all around Huntsville and see where the federal defenses are, what kind they have—breastworks or trenches—and where the artillery pieces are located. See if you can figure out how many troops remain in town. And of course it would be quite helpful to know what the federals plan to do next."

"And how am I supposed to find *that* out?" Lucinda asked, although she knew she already had at least one federal contact.

"Perhaps you can't, but even a small scrap of information could help us retake Huntsville."

"I wouldn't make a very good spy," Lucinda said hesitantly.

"You'd be good at it, because who would suspect a lovely young lady? I won't go back without some information. You can do our cause—and the people of Huntsville—a great deal of good."

"Maybe so, but I can't very well leave here until Aunt Millie gets an overseer or is able to look after things again on her own."

Ben nodded. "I understand that. Also, for their protection, no one else must know what I have asked you to do—that includes your aunt, your father, and my folks, too."

Lucinda was silent, considering his words. "I've never felt comfortable with deceit," she said finally.

"I don't expect you to, but this is different," Ben said. "These are far from normal times. Oh, if only—" he began, then broke off and reached out for Lucinda, pulling her into his arms and laying his head gently against hers. "I wish I could hold you like this forever," he said, so softly that she could scarcely hear.

Lucinda sat quietly, her head against Ben's chest. She heard the measured beat of his heart and felt the warmth of his embrace. Yet she felt strangely detached as his arms tightened around her. For a moment Lucinda sat still, then she pulled away from him and stood.

Ben dropped his arms to his sides and recoiled almost as if she had slapped him. "Forgive me, Lucinda. Seeing you again like this—"

"I have to go now," she said turning from his searching gaze.

"Goodbye, then. I know you'll do what is right," Ben added as he touched her cheek in a tender gesture of farewell.

The other men regarded Lucinda admiringly as she left the cabin and began the walk back to Highmeadows. Ben's words echoed in her mind. *I know you'll do what is right.* Certainly she had a duty to help as many people as she could, to free them from the yoke of bondage imposed by the federals. She couldn't possibly turn her back on Ben now.

Rufe returned in the early afternoon, bringing letters from town.

"Your father sends his love," Millie said, skimming her letter. "He says he thinks there's a tenant at Belle Mina who might be willing to finish out the year here. He's asked Frank Allison to contact him."

Millie put down the letter and sighed. "I had hoped he'd

say that someone was already on the way so you could go on home. I know you'll be glad to give up your new job."

"No more than you will be to be independent again," Lucinda replied. "Isn't there another letter with Papa's?"

"Oh, so there is," Millie replied, holding it up. "It's addressed to you, and not in Arnold's hand."

As she took the paper, Lucinda instantly recognized Major Russell's handwriting. Breaking the sealing wax and unfolding it, she found an undated pass to allow Miss Lucinda Matthews and one servant to go freely from the plantation known as Highmeadows to her residence on Adams Street. A separate note read, "I am truly sorry for the problems you have been caused. Please do not hesitate to call on me if I can serve you in any way. Seth Russell."

"Well, I'm not surprised," Millie said when Lucinda read it to her. "You've certainly bewitched that man."

"I doubt that," Lucinda replied, unwilling to explore the topic further, "but I'm glad to have the pass. It'll make traveling much easier." *And spying.*

"You must feel free to use that pass whenever you want to," Millie said. "I'm improving daily, and you've put things in such great shape that I'm sure I could manage."

"Sorry, but you can't get rid of me so easily. Until someone better comes along, I intend to remain your overseer."

The next day Lucinda again went to the cabin early in the morning, and this time Ben opened the door himself. Entering, she saw that he was alone.

"Where are the others?"

"Out. You don't need to be concerned about it."

"But it does concern me. Aunt Millie and I are both

afraid that the federals are going to find you. She wants to know when you plan to leave."

"That depends on you. You will gather some information for us, I hope?"

"Of course, but I don't know when I can start. You're putting both Aunt Millie and yourselves in danger by staying here. Surely there must be some other place you could go."

"There's a big guerrilla camp not too far from here, but if we go there, you couldn't find me. It's unlikely that the federals would stumble on this cabin."

"I hope you're right," Lucinda said, unconvinced.

"Don't worry about us. Keep your ears open around the federals' headquarters—you might overhear something that would be of great help. But don't write anything down, whatever you do."

"All right. There's enough food here for a couple days. I'll bring more when you need it."

"I'll be waiting." Ben grinned, looking for a moment almost like the carefree boy who had been so happy to go to war.

The next day, a poorly dressed, middle-aged stranger rode up to the house, sent, he said, by Frank Allison.

"I'm Will Graves. Do you still need an overseer, ma'am?" he asked when he had been brought into the parlor to meet Millie.

Millie quickly assured him that he did, and when Lucinda came in from her daily visit to the slave quarters, she found that Mr. Graves had already moved into the overseer's house.

"Well, what do you think?" Lucinda asked her aunt. "Will he do?"

"Lucifer himself would do right now, but the man seems to know what he's about. He's never run a place the size of Highmeadows, but the work's the same and Frank Allison's recommendation was certainly glowing enough. Oh, before I forget it, here's a letter he brought for you. It must be from Alice Ann."

"It seems ages since we last saw each other," Lucinda said, taking the letter eagerly.

"Then run along and read it. I'll be going over the books with Mr. Graves in a little while."

In the privacy of her room, Lucinda kicked off her slippers and sat cross-legged on the counterpane, unconsciously adopting the posture in which she and Alice Ann had so often held lengthy conversations. The letter from her friend was several pages long and had been written over a period of several weeks.

Alice Ann wrote of hating the "terrible peace and quiet" of the country and of trying to persuade her father to let her come to town for a visit. Another portion of the letter expressed surprise that Lucinda was at Highmeadows and added, "I suppose you are as bored with the country as I am," a comment that made Lucinda smile. But the final line, written in a hurried scrawl, quickly erased her smile.

"Word today that Aaron has been wounded—no details. Pray for us."

Lucinda sat holding the letter for a long moment. Her heart went out to Alice Ann and her family. Aaron and Henry had always been friends, going to school together and then joining the same regiment. If Aaron had been wounded, what might have happened to Henry?

Lucinda slid off the bed and ran downstairs in her stocking feet to tell Aunt Millie the news.

"You must go home immediately," Millie said. "When you find out anything more, let me know at once. Aaron and Henry were always so close."

Lucinda comforted her aunt as well as she could in her own distress. "I'll stay a few days longer, to help Mr. Graves settle in," she offered, but Millie wouldn't hear of it.

"Now that I have an overseer and my foot is almost good as new, you really have no reason to stay here."

And I have a very good reason to go, Lucinda thought. Aloud, she said, "Ben and his friends will need more stores in a few days."

"Amos can see to them—don't worry about that. Anyway, I'm sure they will leave soon."

"I'll have Safira get my things together, then."

Lucinda put on her bonnet and took the familiar path to the cabin, perhaps for the last time in some days. No one came to the door when she knocked, and peering in at the dirty window, Lucinda saw no evidence that anyone had ever been there. Apparently Ben and his companions had taken the precaution of storing their quilts and boxes out of sight. Their rifles were gone, too.

Almost as relieved as disappointed that she wouldn't be able to tell Ben goodbye, Lucinda walked back to the house through the woods, thinking how she should carry out his assignment.

seven

"I'll be back soon," Lucinda promised the next morning.

Millie had come outside to see her off, trying hard to look cheerful. "Send word the instant you have news of Henry," she said, and Lucinda nodded.

"Watch out for that foot," Lucinda cautioned as she mounted Ginger and adjusted her riding dress around the pommel of her sidesaddle.

"Don't worry. I've learned my lesson. Be careful, now."

With a final wave, Lucinda turned Ginger toward the lane leading back to the main road. This time Rufe rode Millie's roan mare so they could make better time. Her pass from Major Russell would come in very handy, Lucinda thought as she turned Ginger south onto the Winchester Pike. She might need to make more than one trip back to Highmeadows before Ben had all the information he needed, and it would be awkward to have to explain each errand at General Mitchell's headquarters.

"We all gwine to miss you, Miss Lucinda," Rufe said after they had ridden for some minutes in silence.

"I'll miss Highmeadows, too," Lucinda replied, and in a way she would. Her hard work there had given her a welcome sense of purpose. *But I have another purpose now,* she reminded herself.

They had covered only a few miles when the first faint sounds of what was quite clearly gunfire came from somewhere to the east.

"Do you hear that?" Lucinda asked Rufe.

"Yes'm. I 'spect the Yankees is chasing some folks.

"We must be 'bout even with the Camden settlement."

Lucinda looked toward the mountains, trying to imagine how anyone could ride and fire in such steep terrain. On the other side of the mountain ran the main east-west railroad track.

"I b'lieve they's comin' this way," Rufe said as the sounds grew louder, and Lucinda began to look around for a hiding place. They had been riding through cultivated land with little cover, but just ahead and to the right she saw a cotton gin.

"Let's get to shelter," she said, pointing toward the building and urging Ginger forward. The distance could not have been more than a half mile, but it seemed to take forever to cover. Worse, the tracks their horses made in the fresh mud pointed directly at them.

"I hope they don't look this way," Lucinda said as the shots grew even closer.

Suddenly several horsemen broke from the wooded edge of the mountain and galloped through the adjacent fields, crossing the road Lucinda and Rufe had left only moments before. From the distance that separated them, Lucinda couldn't tell much about the riders except that they weren't wearing any sort of regular uniforms. Hats obscured their faces, but for a split-second Lucinda saw— or imagined—a flash of blond beard as the men disappeared into a field on the western side of the road.

Moments later, a troop of a dozen or so blue-uniformed soldiers appeared in hot pursuit and also crossed the road, too intent on their quarry to take any notice of Lucinda and Rufe.

"That was close," Lucinda said when the men in blue had also ridden out of sight. "I wonder who they were chasing?" she asked, afraid she already knew the answer.

She thought of Ben's mysterious absences and the weapons she had seen at the cabin. While waiting for her to bring intelligence, he evidently wasn't being idle. The knowledge that he was tangling with Yankees disturbed her. *The sooner he gets information from me, the sooner they'll be out of this,* Lucinda told herself.

"They ain't no tellin' who-all the Yankees will chase," Rufe said, his tone making it clear that he wanted no part of them.

"Well, whoever they are, I hope they get away. I suppose it's safe to go on now."

The rest of their trip proceeded without incident. The pickets all accepted Lucinda's pass without question. She noted the pickets' locations, although she was certain that Ben already knew quite well where the perimeter guards were posted.

Huntsville looked the same, yet strangely different as they rode back into town. The areas around Maple Hill Cemetery and Echols Hill had been so fortified as to be almost unrecognizable. She'd have to come back for a closer look at that, Lucinda decided. Adams Street was still crowded with federal soldiers as she and Rufe turned into it.

With relief, Lucinda stepped down to the mounting block and handed Ginger's reins to Rufe. Her riding dress was spattered with mud, and she paused to brush off the worst of it before unlatching the gate. Lucinda had just started up the walk when the front door opened. She smiled, thinking that her father, Lige, or Viola had seen her, but instead a man in a blue uniform came out of the house toward her.

So the house has been taken, after all, was Lucinda's first thought. Her second was that her father must have been arrested. Then the man removed his hat, and Lucinda recognized Major Russell. The thought that she was glad to see him she credited to relief.

"Good evening, Miss Matthews. I trust you had a pleasant visit with your aunt?"

Lucinda wondered if this man had any idea of what running a plantation involved. But of course he didn't. He'd told her he was a city-bred lawyer, and it was not her place to enlighten him.

"Yes," Lucinda said, careful not to return his smile. "Is my father at home?"

"No, and I have a matter of some urgency to discuss with him. When he comes in, he should call on me as soon as possible."

"At the McDowell's—I mean, General Mitchel's headquarters?"

"No, I'll be at my quarters at the Allison house."

At the mention of her friends, Lucinda's mouth tightened, an expression he read well.

"I can assure you that my staff and I haven't harmed the house or property," he said.

"The Allisons will be glad to hear that, especially since they've just received some very bad news."

"Oh?" The major's eyebrows lifted questioningly, and thinking that it could do no harm, Lucinda told him about Alice Ann's report that her brother had been wounded.

"I'm sorry," he said, politely.

He doesn't mean it, Lucinda thought. *He doesn't know*

them, and one more Rebel soldier wounded is just one less he has to fight. They were enemies, and no amount of politeness could ever change that.

"Excuse me, Major, but I'm tired, and I would like to go inside," Lucinda said when it became obvious that he was in no hurry to depart.

"Certainly," he said, and offered her his arm as if she might not be able to make it the last few yards up her walk. "Did you have any trouble with the pickets?" he asked, subtly reminding Lucinda of his favor to her.

"No, Major," she said, formally polite. She saw no reason to tell him about the skirmish she and Rufe had come upon; such patrols were no doubt routine, and no doubt he'd learn about it soon enough.

"Are you home to stay now?"

They reached the door and the major looked into Lucinda's eyes as if some other answer might be found there. The intensity of his expression, so much like Ben's, made Lucinda feel uncomfortable, then annoyed.

"I'll probably return soon to check on my aunt," she managed to say, directing her gaze to the metal buttons on his coat, level with her eyes. For the first time, she noticed that each button was a miniature of the great shield of the United States. An eagle grasped lightning bolts in one talon and an olive branch in the other. The federals had shown the lightning well enough, but not the olive branch, she thought with fine irrelevance. Lucinda couldn't look into his eyes—it was too dangerous.

"She is fortunate to have such devotion. Don't forget to remind Mr. Matthews that I need to see him. Good evening." The major half-bowed before he turned and walked away.

Lucinda felt uneasy, recalling her aunt's declaration that Major Russell was up to something. *Well, so am I,* she thought. Perhaps she could put the major's interest in her to good use, but at the moment Lucinda felt too tired to think about it.

After she had bathed and donned a fresh dress, Lucinda came down the stairs just as her father entered the house. Immediately she noticed that he seemed changed. Had his hair always been so gray? And surely the lines in his face had deepened. But he brightened when he saw his daughter.

"Ah, Lucinda. I was ready to come after you if you hadn't come home."

"And I was ready to come back. Have you any news of Henry yet? Alice Ann wrote that Aaron had been wounded."

"Yes, Aaron took a minnie ball in his thigh. We still haven't heard from Henry, but I take that to be good news."

"Well, I don't. Until I see him walk in that door again, I'll not stop praying for him."

"Tell me about Highmeadows. I take it that Allison's man got there all right, since you're back."

"Yes, he came yesterday, and I believe he'll do a good job. Aunt Millie's foot has healed so well that she's now able to keep in touch with everything."

"Good. I'm glad Millie's better and even happier that you didn't have to stay longer."

"I'll be going back soon," Lucinda put in quickly. "I promised Aunt Millie that I would. Besides, I want to make sure that Mr. Graves is working out."

Mr. Matthews frowned. "I don't want you out on the roads. From all I hear, it isn't safe."

If only you knew, Papa, Lucinda thought. She hadn't written him about her encounter with the federal soldiers or Major Russell's part in rescuing her, and apparently the major hadn't mentioned it either. Thus reminded of Major Russell, Lucinda relayed his message.

"He said for you to come to the Allison house on a matter of some urgency—he didn't say what it concerned."

Arnold Matthews rose from his chair with great reluctance. "Get some rest. You look pretty well done in. I hope to be back soon."

He was gone for half an hour, and when he returned, Lucinda's father looked grim.

"The major thought I should know that several of our most prominent citizens will be arrested tomorrow."

"Who—and on what grounds?" Lucinda asked, the old alarm about her father's safety sounding again.

"He didn't mention any names, but I've a pretty fair idea. Some are suspected of helping the guerrillas, while others refused to take the oath of allegiance."

"And are you to be detained, as well?"

"Not to his knowledge. I haven't been asked to sign the oath, for some reason. If I were to be asked and refused, then I would probably be detained for a time also. But I doubt that the arrests will be widespread. The major is quite aware that keeping the people of Huntsville stirred up doesn't help the federals, either. I hope that General Mitchel will listen to him. Rumor says that Morgan or Kirby-Smith are on their way here, but so far nothing has come of it except for a few skirmishes along the railroad line."

I know all about that, Lucinda thought, but she didn't intend to burden her father further by telling him what she and Rufe had seen. He'd never allow her to return to Highmeadows if he knew how close she had come to being part of the action.

"Speaking of letters," she said aloud, "hearing from Alice Ann has made me want to see her again. Do you think that Aunt Dora and Uncle Frank would let her come back and stay with us for a few days?"

"They might. Write them, and I'll ask the major for a pass to send with the letter."

That evening Lucinda wrote the Allisons a brief note, expressing sympathy to the family about Aaron's being wounded and inviting Alice Ann to come to Huntsville for a visit. Then she excused herself and went up to bed before it was fully dark.

Tired as she was, Lucinda couldn't fall asleep. Accustomed to the featherbed at Highmeadows, her own bed felt strange and uncomfortable, and she kept thinking about how she could complete the mission Ben had given her.

The June air was heavy and the sun glowed like copper in a dusty, hazy sky, promising another hot day as Lucinda and her father walked to church the next day.

"We'll see no rain today," Mr. Matthews predicted.

"It's good cotton weather," Lucinda replied absently. Aware that she might see Ben's parents at church, she wished he hadn't forbidden her to tell them she had seen him. If she were in his position, she would want her father to know she was all right.

As they entered the sanctuary, Lucinda saw that the Bradleys were already seated, and nothing in their expressions or behavior seemed the slightest bit unusual. After nodding to them, Lucinda looked over at the visitors' pew, where she was unsurprised to see Major Russell seated with two other officers, just as they had been on Easter. Somehow she'd known he'd be there. He nodded and smiled at her, but Lucinda flushed and turned away, barely acknowledging his greeting.

As if he were determined to ignore the alien presence in his congregation, Pastor Ross opened the huge old pulpit Bible and began to read from Romans eight. Lucinda had heard the passage before, but today the words seemed more meaningful for a congregation encircled by its enemies.

"If God be for us, who can be against us?. . . Who shall separate us from the love of Christ? shall tribulation, or distress, or persecution, or famine, or nakedness, or peril, or sword?. . . For thy sake we are killed all the day long; we are accounted as sheep before the slaughter. Nay, in all these things we are more than conquerors through him that loved us."

No matter who might win earthly battles, Pastor Ross said, Christians would always be more than conquerors because of the love of God in sending His Son Jesus to earth.

More than conquerors. Lucinda marked the place in her Testament and resolved to underline the passage in her bedside Bible.

The sermon had been well-received by the church members, but Lucinda saw that those it might trouble had again disappeared the moment the service ended. When she went outside, she found Mrs. Bradley waiting for her near the steps.

"It's good to have you back home, Lucinda. Did you enjoy your stay in the country?"

"It wasn't exactly a pleasure trip. I expect to return soon."

"That might be dangerous. Have you heard the news about Ben?" she added, lowering her voice.

Lucinda's heart skipped a beat. "No, ma'am. Has something happened to him?"

"He's been seen with the guerrillas, right here in Madison County. I thought perhaps he might have contacted you."

"Ollice Kinnard brought me a letter from him on Easter Sunday," Lucinda said, choosing an old truth over a new lie.

"Well, if you hear from Ben, please let us know. We were worried before, of course, but now. . . ."

Her sentence needed no finishing, and Lucinda was relieved when her father broke away from his conversation and said it was time to leave. She was still wishing she could have reassured Mrs. Bradley when she saw Major Russell, apparently waiting for them at the next intersection.

"Tell me, Major," Mr. Matthews said in greeting, "how did you find the service today? Or perhaps your visit was strictly official?"

"I was asked to monitor a church service," he replied, "but I specifically asked to attend your church."

"And what will you report?"

"I found nothing seditious in the minister's remarks, but I must confess I did not follow his line of reasoning." As he spoke, Seth looked directly at Lucinda. "Perhaps you can enlighten me, Miss Matthews."

What?" Arnold Matthews asked, looking surprised.

"Perhaps you aren't aware that your daughter disputes

theology with a vigor equal to the Reverend's. Some day I'd like to continue our conversation, Miss Matthews."

Lucinda colored under her father's questioning glance. "I believe I said all I had to say at the time."

"Then that is my loss, Miss Matthews. Good day, sir, ma'am," Seth said smoothly, nodding to them as he turned toward the Allison house.

"What was that all about?" her father asked. "I wasn't aware that you and Major Russell had any occasion for conversation."

"He came to Highmeadows," she said, again speaking the truth after a fashion.

"Major Russell is a better man than most of the federals, but take care around him, Lucinda."

"You use him when it suits your purposes," Lucinda said. "Do you think that's right?"

He shrugged. "I do what I must for the benefit of all."

And so shall I, Lucinda thought, fervently wishing that Ben had someone else to spy for him.

In the next few days, always accompanied by either Lige or Viola, Lucinda managed to cover the entire town, making a mental inventory of the artillery she saw and memorizing the kind and location of federal defenses. To her casual question of how many troops her father thought were in Huntsville, he replied, "Too many." And as for finding out the federals' future plans, the only person who might have shared that information with her was nowhere to be seen.

"I haven't seen Major Russell lately," Lucinda said to her father at mid-week. "I suppose that means that things are running more smoothly these days."

"Hardly," he replied. "I just learned that smallpox has

broken out among the federal troops. Everyone in Huntsville is going to have to be protected against it, or we could have a terrible epidemic on our hands."

"Smallpox!" Lucinda shuddered. She had seen people who had survived the disease, and instinctively she put a hand to her face.

"Dr. Sheffey will vaccinate us, but I couldn't persuade anyone at headquarters to talk to me about it today."

"So you didn't see Major Russell?"

"No, or anyone else with authority. When they want something from us, it's a different story, of course."

All that day and the next, Lucinda kept expecting Major Russell to come to see them, but he did not. Their only visitor came from Belle Mina with a reply to Lucinda's invitation. There had been some trouble with bushwhackers, Dora Allison wrote, and although things were presently calm, they needed to stay there. Aaron's wife, Sally Ann, was coming to stay with them.

In a postscript Alice Ann added, "Send me a letter by Sally with all your news."

Knowing that the federal pickets would undoubtedly read her letter, Lucinda dared not reveal anything about Ben, so she truthfully wrote that she had seen very few people and added that the Allison's house was being well-cared for, news she knew they would be glad to hear.

"I can drop your letter off at the Merrick's on my way back to town," Arnold offered after lunch.

"Thank you, but I'll take it myself and visit with Sally."

"Then I'll walk you there, but someone must escort you home."

"Papa! The Merricks live just two blocks away!" Lucinda protested, but he made her promise not to come home alone.

"I don't see many soldiers out these days," Lucinda commented as they walked. "Do you suppose they're all sick?"

"I doubt it. I suspect that many of them may be out hunting for guerrillas."

"How many guerrillas are there, I wonder?" Lucinda asked. She didn't want to think that Ben and his companions were in peril.

"Enough to keep the enemy angry, apparently. But why this sudden interest in warfare? Do you plan to add military strategy to your overseeing skills?"

"Perhaps," Lucinda replied. It was good to see that her father's mood had improved, and she smiled as he waved goodbye.

The Merricks lived in a raised cottage with a double set of curved brick steps leading to a wide front door. Lucinda had barely touched her hand to the brass knocker when Sally appeared and embraced her.

Sally was pale and thin, the dark smudges under her eyes mute evidence of recent sleepless nights. She seemed almost pathetically glad to see Lucinda, and her eyes glowed as she showed Lucinda a letter she had just received from her husband. Although Henry's name wasn't mentioned, Aaron had said that "all the Huntsville boys" were still together and fit. The letter had arrived in the first batch of mail the federals had allowed into the city, and Sally thought it must have been written just before the battle in which Aaron had been wounded.

"Then we may hear from Henry any day now!" Lucinda exclaimed, cheered by the prospect. Lucinda visited with Sally for over an hour, then rose to go.

"I'll send Eula with you," Sally said. She called her maid, a girl scarcely their age.

"She's no bigger than I am," Lucinda said when she saw Eula, "but to please Papa, I'll let her walk home with me."

The afternoon sun was beginning to cast shadows as they walked down White Street and crossed to Adams Street. They met no one until they had almost reached Lucinda's house and saw three Union soldiers leaning against the wall in front of the house across the street. The men stared but said nothing as Lucinda and Eula passed, both directing their eyes straight ahead.

At her gate, Lucinda thanked Eula for walking with her. "I think you should go home the back way," she added, aware that the soldiers still watched them.

"Yes'm, Miss Lucinda," Eula replied. She followed Lucinda around the house to the side veranda, where Lucinda entered through the french doors and Eula kept walking toward the alley leading to White Street.

Lucinda hung her bonnet on the hall tree and glanced out the front parlor window. Seeing that the soldiers were no longer across the street, she dismissed them from her mind and started up the stairs.

Suddenly, ear-piercing screams erupted from behind the house. Lucinda ran outside, calling for Lige to come with her. He had been working in the vegetable garden on the other side of the house and immediately followed her, a pointed trowel in one hand.

The shrieks came from the alley, and even before they reached it, Lucinda feared the worst. A federal soldier on either side of her held Eula's arms, while the third forced her to the ground. Her apron had been torn off, and scratches on the face of one of the men testified to the intensity of her struggle.

"Let her go!" Lucinda cried, grabbing the sleeve of the nearest soldier. She pulled so hard that the fabric ripped, but the man paid her no heed. "Lige, do something!" she yelled, flailing at another soldier.

When Lige raised the trowel to hit one of the men, another turned and wrenched it from him, then began striking him with it. Lucinda's screams were added to Eula's, then to Viola's as she came out to investigate the commotion.

"What is all of this caterwauling?" another federal soldier demanded, arriving at the scene with his rifle pointed at them.

Eula's assailants let her go and scowled at Lucinda.

"These men attacked this girl," Lucinda said, "and when we tried to stop them, they beat my servant."

The soldier looked from the sobbing girl to Lige's bloody face and lowered his weapon. "Come with me to headquarters. I'll have to make an incident report."

Lucinda knew about incident reports. All sorts of outrages had been performed by the federals, and usually all that ever happened was that a report was filed and forgotten. Very seldom were the perpetrators identified or punished. Reluctantly, Lucinda went along to headquarters where she and the three servants were left waiting with a guard. The federals who had caused the trouble had simply walked away and were nowhere in sight.

"Miz Sally gwine ter have my hide," Eula mourned, looking at her torn dress.

"It's all right, Eula. I'll explain everything to Miss Sally," Lucinda said. "Try to stop crying."

Viola made some effort to calm the girl, then turned her

attention to Lige's wounds. His face bore several shallow cuts, and one eye was rapidly swelling shut.

"This man needs medical attention," Lucinda told the guard as the minutes slowly passed. "I demand to see Major Russell."

At the mention of the major's name, the guard, a lean and angular man of perhaps thirty-five, shifted his tobacco chaw and grinned humorlessly. "I don't reckon he wants to see you, though, ma'am."

"Then let us go," Lucinda said, softening her tone. "We've done nothing wrong."

"That ain't for you to say," the guard declared, and looked the other way.

Another fifteen minutes passed before the soldier who had brought them to headquarters finally reappeared and told them to follow him. They were led past the room where Lucinda had been given her pass to Highmeadows and into what had been the family dining room. A tired-looking man looked up as they entered.

"I would like to see Major Russell," Lucinda said, attempting to make herself as tall and imposing as possible.

"Major Russell has nothing to do with this matter. I'm Captain Warren, the duty officer. You'll deal with me."

"Why don't you let him make that decision?" Lucinda asked, trying not to show her rising anger.

"Because that's *my* decision," Captain Warren said. "Why are these people here, Corporal?"

After hearing the soldier's account, the captain asked a series of questions about the incident, which Lucinda answered as the others stood in frightened silence.

"Assaulting federal soldiers is a grave offense. But

considering the circumstances, I'll overlook it if you'll sign the loyalty oath and vow that you won't interfere with the federal government and its representatives again. Do that, and you'll be free to go."

"And what if I don't?" Lucinda asked, hardly believing her ears.

"Well, then, you won't be released," he said matter-of-factly.

"I ain't 'saulted nobody," Viola said, speaking for the first time.

"Me, neither," Eula added in a strangled voice. Her crying had brought on an attack of hiccoughs which provided a bizarre punctuation to the strange interview.

"What about the men who attacked this girl?" Lucinda asked. "Why don't you arrest them?"

"What the United States Army does with its own is not your concern," the soldier said, his eyes narrowing. "Now I'll ask you just one more time: Will you swear these oaths or not?"

Lucinda took a deep breath and looked at Viola. Her eyes burned with anger, but she said nothing. Lige stood impassively, his swollen eye making him appear to be winking grotesquely. Eula sniveled and hiccoughed softly. All three looked miserable and obviously wanted to be out of federal hands as soon as possible.

"What about them?" Lucinda asked. "Are they to be allowed to go?"

"If they'll agree to leave our men alone, yes. Come, now, you're wasting my time. Will you cooperate or not?"

Lucinda thought of what her father had said about listening to her conscience and turned to Viola. "I can't do what this man wants, but you all can and should. Say what he wants you to and take Eula home."

"But Miss Lucinda, we can't leave you here with all of these—with the soldiers," Viola protested.

"It's all right," Lucinda assured her. "I'll be along in a little while. If I'm not home by supper time, you'll know what to tell Papa."

Viola looked at Lige, who nodded, and the three slaves mumbled a promise not to harm any representatives of the federal government and were immediately ushered from the room.

"Well, Miss Sesech," Captain Warren said, "now that your slaves have deserted you, perhaps you'll change your tune, eh?"

Lucinda shook her head, and the man sighed.

"All right, missy, you had your chance. Maybe a spell in jail will change your mind."

Jail? Lucinda heard the word without quite comprehending it. She had assumed she'd be kept waiting at headquarters until someone—preferably Major Russell—saw what was happening and let her go. She certainly hadn't thought she'd be locked up.

"Where are you taking me?" she asked, but there was no answer.

In short order, Lucinda was put into a closed carriage for a ride to a house several streets away. She recognized it as belonging to the Moores, who'd crossed the Tennessee River shortly after the federals came. Apparently, the house had been turned into a makeshift jail. Lucinda was ushered inside and all but shoved into a room at the head of a flight of stairs. Then her escort withdrew, locked the door from the outside, and left her alone.

The room was dark, its single window covered with

shutters that were closed and fastened from the outside so she couldn't see out. The chamber contained a narrow cot with a lumpy, dirty mattress, a small table without a candle or lamp, and a bowl and pitcher.

Lucinda sat on the mattress and tried to realize that she really was being held against her will. Her righteous indignation had subsided, but the sense of outrage which had gotten her into the situation told her she had done the right thing.

Soon, she thought, her father would find out what had happened and see that she was released. Lucinda allowed her mind to roam a bit, imagining her father bursting in on Major Russell with the news of her arrest, and the major himself coming for her. He would open the door and beg her to forgive them, and she would—

In her pleasant fantasy, Lucinda thought she might allow the major to embrace her when he freed her from her unjust captivity. He'd be contrite about her imprisonment, and in response he would gladly tell her all the secrets of Huntsville's defenses.

But Lucinda's dreams faded with the dying daylight as no one came to her rescue. Her stomach rumbled, reminding her that she had missed supper. Outside the nighttime chorus of tree frogs and crickets masked any sounds she might have heard in the house. Several times she thought she heard footsteps outside her door, but they didn't stop, and no one entered.

The room grew cool with the darkness, and Lucinda wrestled the window shut, cutting out some of the noise but only a part of the chill. Shivering, she curled into a miserable ball and fervently wished she could stop time and go back to the afternoon, before any of this happened.

If only she hadn't decided to see Sally! Yet what had happened had an almost fated quality. The soldiers who had attacked Eula could have done so at any time, and if she hadn't been there to hear the girl's screams. . . .

Lucinda didn't want to think what would have happened if she hadn't come to Eula's aid. It could have happened to her, too, she realized. The drunken sergeant's face came into her mind, and she shuddered as she imagined his hands pawing her body. Anyway, Lucinda reasoned, forcing her mind away from its morbid imaginings, the main thing was that the federal soldiers had no right to behave as they had. If anyone was put into jail, it should be the men who committed the outrage, not the one who had sought to prevent it. Surely the logic of the situation would eventually prevail, even among Yankees.

Eventually, warmed a bit by her wrath and consoled by the thought that she would certainly be released soon, Lucinda fell asleep.

"You say that Miss Matthews has been *arrested*?" Seth asked, trying to comprehend what Private O'Brien was telling him. "Whatever for?"

"She wouldn't promise not to attack representatives of the federal government," the private said, grinning as he recalled the look on the girl's face. "She sure was mad."

It was barely dawn, and Seth had just returned to the Allison house, tired and muddy. He unbelted his extra ammunition cartridges and stared at his aide in disbelief.

"Where is she being held?" he asked, but the private didn't know.

Seth debated his best course of action. The idea of Lucinda's being imprisoned was almost ridiculous, but after hearing the charges, he wasn't surprised that she had been detained. He knew the flinty determination that had appealed to him from the first moment he saw her was quite capable of causing Lucinda trouble.

"Bring me a cup of coffee," he ordered his aide.

"What are you going to do, sir?"

"I'm going to have my breakfast, Private. Then I must rescue a damsel in distress."

eight

Lucinda awoke with the dawn and for a moment didn't recognize her surroundings. Then the memory of the day before came flooding back, and she groaned. It was still cool in the room, and when she tried to stand, she discovered that her joints were stiff and she felt lightheaded. It occurred to her that she hadn't eaten in a long time, and she pounded on the closed, locked door of her room.

"Is anybody there?" she cried and felt momentary panic when no one answered. She again beat on the door, this time using her shoe, and soon afterward she heard approaching footsteps.

"Quiet!" a rough male voice cried in reply.

"I'm hungry," Lucinda said, trying to speak loudly enough to be heard through the thick wooden door. "Don't you feed your prisoners?"

"Only the purty gals," the voice replied, and Lucinda stood back as a key grated in the lock.

A burly sergeant opened the door just wide enough to hand her a pitcher of water and a scrap of linen. "I heard we had a special guest," he said, ogling her. "Our visitors usually bring their own vittles, but I'll see what I can find."

"My father will bring food to me," Lucinda said. "Arnold Matthews—across and down Adams Street from headquarters. Please tell him—"

But the man had already closed the door and retreated,

135

his boots rasping on the uncarpeted stairway.

Lucinda might be at the mercy of the rough man, but she was determined not to let him think she feared him. She washed as well as she could in cold water that made her shiver, then knelt and prayed for strength. In a little while, the sergeant returned with a bowl of cornmeal mush and a crust of hard bread.

After she finished eating, Lucinda went to the window and tried to look through the cracks in the shutters, but they were angled in such a way that she could see nothing. For some minutes she paced the floor, partly for exercise but mostly for something to do. At first, sure that at any moment she would be released, she strained her ears listening for evidence that someone had come for her. But as time passed and all remained quiet below, she grew increasingly uneasy.

As the morning wore on, she wondered why Seth Russell hadn't been to see her. He must know about her arrest—it was probably all over town by now. Maybe, she thought with some discomfort, she'd been mistaken in believing that the major was attracted to her. Or—the thought brought a thrill of alarm—perhaps something had happened to him.

Lucinda recalled the skirmish she'd witnessed on her way home. Was Seth at Highmeadows even now, finding Ben and his friends? So absorbed was Lucinda in her dark thoughts that she didn't hear the footsteps on the stairs. But then a key rattled in the lock, and she looked hopefully toward the door. Could it be her father, at last? Or, more than likely, she told herself, her guard was just returning for her plate. Then the door swung open, admitting Seth Russell.

For an instant neither spoke, then both started to speak at once before they lapsed into an awkward silence. Contrary to her fantasy of the evening before, which now seemed quite ridiculous, Lucinda did not throw herself into the major's arms, nor did he make any move to embrace her. Her initial reaction was surprise at his unkempt appearance. He obviously hadn't shaved that morning, and his uniform was stained with dried red clay.

For his part, Seth was surprised at the austere conditions under which Lucinda was being held, but not at her composure. From what he had learned about Lucinda, he hadn't expected to find her in hysterics.

"I had some trouble locating you," he said after a moment. "I trust that you haven't been mistreated?"

Lucinda folded her arms and attempted to glare at him. "The fact that I'm here in the first place is mistreatment enough. I certainly hope you're here to take me home."

Seth shook his head and took a step forward. "I'm sorry, but I'm afraid you'll have to stay here a while."

A wave of disappointment washed over Lucinda, and Seth's sympathetic glance only irritated her more. "Do you think that I'm that dangerous, Major?"

You've endangered my heart, at least, Seth thought. He smiled, bringing color to her cheeks. "I'm told that you put up a pretty good fight before you were arrested."

"I just wish I could've done more! You weren't there, Major. You didn't see how those men attacked that defenseless slave girl, then turned on us when we tried to help her."

Seth sighed and folded his arms across his chest. "I'm sure you did what you thought you had to, Miss Matthews, but by refusing to say that you'd do no harm to federal troops, you upset General Mitchel. He intends to make an example of you in the hope that the townspeople will give us a little more respect—"

"Respect!" Lucinda interrupted. "How can that man speak of respect while allowing his troops to run wild?"

That's just the way you looked the first time I saw you, Seth thought, admiring the determined jut of Lucinda's chin. He tried to sound stern as he spoke aloud. "It's a good thing he can't hear you say that. Believe me, I'll do what I can to gain your release, but in the meantime, what do you need?"

Lucinda's gesture took in the room where they stood. "Linen and a blanket for the cot, a lantern, some clothing—and my Bible."

"I'll see that you get them. Is there anything else?"

"Does my father know where I am?"

"I doubt it, but I'll tell him and leave word that he can visit you and bring what you need."

"Thank you, Major. I really do want to go home," she added as he turned to leave.

From the doorway, he nodded. "I know. Goodbye, Miss Lucinda."

After he left, Lucinda sat on the cot and thought about her promise to Ben. Each day he stayed at Highmeadows put him in more danger. If she didn't get back soon, Lucinda thought, she'd have to find someone to take the information she had gathered.

That afternoon General Mitchel and his adjutant bent over a map in the general's office, and Seth pointed to an area north of the hamlet of Camden. "From all reports, the guerrillas' camp is somewhere in this area, sir. I believe we were close to it last night."

"I want that camp wiped out. Form a patrol and find it."

"Yes, sir. And General...," Seth hesitated, then plunged on as the general raised his head and looked at him. "When I get back, perhaps we can discuss releasing Miss Matthews."

General Mitchel frowned. "That discussion is over, Major. Go on now, and report to me as soon as you return, no matter how late the hour."

When Arnold Matthews came to see Lucinda later that day, he brought everything she had requested, expressed his anger at her arrest, and then gave her some welcome news.

"Henry has finally written us, and he's all right."

Her brother's letter described Aaron's wound as bad enough to invalid him for a time, but unlikely to cause permanent damage or disfigurement. He himself hadn't been wounded, he emphasized, and was doing as well as anyone could in their circumstances. He didn't reveal where their outfit was located, but he made an oblique reference to his family's situation, writing that he hoped the "new way" they were living was "tolerable." He concluded with a statement that Lucinda found oddly touching in a young man barely twenty years old. "Don't worry about me. I won't die before my time."

"I always felt deep down that Henry was all right," Lucinda said after reading his letter.

"So did I, but after hearing that Aaron had been wounded, I began to have my doubts. His letter comes at a good time."

After her father left, Lucinda half-expected Major

Russell to pay her a return visit, and when no one else was admitted to her room, her disappointment both surprised and annoyed her. *But of course the general's adjutant was a busy man,* Lucinda told herself. He'd be back to see her. She knew it.

The next day, in place of her father, Lucinda received an unexpected visitor.

"Aunt Millie!" she exclaimed, scarcely able to believe her eyes. "Has something happened?" she asked, fearing the worst.

"The overseer is working out well, and my foot is good as new."

"I can't believe you actually left Highmeadows," Lucinda said.

"I had a reason," Millie said, lowering her voice and glancing back at the door as if she feared being overheard. "Does it concern Ben?" Lucinda asked, and Millie nodded.

"He and the other soldiers left the cabin a few days ago—or at least I thought they had gone. Amos came back and indicated that no one was there two days in a row when he took food for them.

"But then two nights ago, Ben Bradley came up to the house after midnight and threw pebbles at my window. I went down, and he asked if I knew when you were coming back. When I told him I didn't, he said you were supposed to be bringing some information that they needed right away. He seemed so intent about it that I promised to come to town and let you know. He promises to leave Highmeadows for good as soon as he hears from you."

"I'm sorry he bothered you about it," Lucinda said,

somewhat surprised that he had.

"Well, I don't mind, but I wish you'd told me what was going on before you left. I wasn't aware that you and Ben knew each other so well," she added, giving Lucinda a meaningful glance. "He's quite concerned about you."

"Or maybe he's just concerned about my information. He thought it best you not know what I was doing, since it would only worry you."

"That's true enough. And I soon realized that your father isn't aware of your plans to help the boys."

Lucinda nodded. "That's right, and it would serve no useful purpose to tell him, either."

"I agree. Did trying to get Ben's information have anything to do with your arrest?"

"No. What Papa told you is the whole story. No one could possibly know that I'd been gathering information for Ben. I was very careful."

Millie smiled ruefully. "So careful you're locked up! It seems that I'll have to go in your place."

"I don't have all he asked for, but I can tell you what I know about the defenses and where the pickets are. And speaking of pickets—how did you manage to get into town without a pass?"

Millie grinned. "Bribery. I told 'em I'd have a pass when I went back home, but in the meantime, they might enjoy some fresh pie I just happened to have with me. They were too busy eating to stop me."

"You shouldn't try to return without a pass, though. See Major Russell at headquarters. He's been very kind to us," she added, seeing Millie's raised eyebrows.

"I told you he was up to something," Millie said. "If he's so kind, why are you still here? Yankees show a strange sort of kindness."

"If it were up to him, I'd be free now, but he lacks the authority to release me. He's seen to it that I have what I need."

"I can believe that," Millie muttered. "Just watch him like a hawk, Lucinda. Now, tell me what to say to Ben."

Seth Russell had chosen his patrol carefully, all seasoned soldiers accustomed to riding at night in unfamiliar territory. But as they made their way into the Paint Rock Valley and began to hear an unusual number of owl calls, he wished he had brought a larger force.

"Take cover," Seth called as he heard a stirring in the woods by the side of the road. It was too late. Desperately, he spurred Star, but three men blocked the road behind them, revolvers glinting in the moonlight.

"Welcome, Yanks," one of them said, and another—a man with a blond beard Seth was sure he had seen before—laughed softly.

"You're looking for our camp, Major? Let's take them there, boys."

Seth's hands were seized and a rough hood, perhaps a doubled burlap bag, covered his head, making the darkness complete.

Lucinda didn't expect to see her aunt again, and she wasn't surprised when her father brought the news the next day that Millie had left early that morning to return to Highmeadows.

"Did she get a pass?"

"Yes. The duty officer—Captain Warren, I believe it was—gave her one. I'm sure he didn't realize she was your aunt."

"That's good," Lucinda said.

"Yes. To have both of you in jail at the same time would be a bit more than I could handle!"

"Have you seen Major Russell lately?" she asked, trying to sound casual.

"No, I haven't. He's probably busy running errands. The general's family has arrived, and furnishings are being taken from a number of places to equip the Clay house to their liking."

"If General Mitchel sent for his family, he must be expecting to stay here a long time," Lucinda said. She wished she'd known that piece of information the day before.

"He may not have the opportunity. The major told me in confidence some time back of certain letters that the general has received from the War Department questioning the effectiveness of his command. He could be replaced at any moment."

"How strange that an enemy officer should share such privileged news!" Lucinda exclaimed.

"Is that how you still think of Major Russell?" her father asked.

"It doesn't matter how I think of him," she replied, lowering her eyes in embarrassment. "He wears the same uniform as the guard that keeps me locked up."

"I'll grant that he does, but without his help we'd have no home, and I'd probably be in prison in Ohio."

And just why do you think he helped us? Lucinda thought, but dared not say.

"If General Mitchel is replaced, do you suppose Major Russell would still be able to help us?" she asked.

"Who knows? We'll have to wait and see. In the meantime, I just pray that he can persuade General Mitchel to release you soon."

On the seventh day of her imprisonment, Lucinda woke early, fully expecting to be set free that day. Surely a week spent in a locked room would be considered punishment enough, she thought. She still hadn't seen Major Russell again, and her longing to do so shamed and irritated her. *It's just because I don't have anything else to think about, stuck here all alone,* she told herself.

When Lucinda heard a faint commotion from downstairs shortly before noon, her first thought was that another prisoner was being brought in to join her and the several others being kept in the house. But something was definitely strange and frightening about the sounds she now heard. Someone pounded up the stairs with a heavy tread and ran down the hall.

Lucinda heard a key grating in the lock of a room across the hall—which as far as she knew was empty—then the steps moved toward her door and a key was fitted to its lock. She looked around the room for a hiding place, but there was none, nor was there anything she could use in self-defense. All Lucinda could do was move away from the door so she would be behind it when it opened.

The door flung open, and Lucinda's eyes widened in surprise as a blond soldier in federal blue entered the room, holding a pistol in his right hand. He whirled around and their eyes met.

"Hurry! We've got to get out of here."

Lucinda's vision blurred for a moment, then cleared as he came closer. "Ben!" she cried. "Wha—"

But he gave her no time to finish her question as he half-led, half-pushed her from the room, down the stairs, past the crumpled figure of the guard, and out into the peaceful sunshine of a summer noon. Ben untied a horse from the hitching post in front of the house and vaulted into the saddle. He reached down and boosted Lucinda up behind him, and she scarcely had time to adjust her skirts before Ben had urged the horse to a fast walk, then to a canter.

"This is insane," Lucinda managed to say as they rounded a corner and started north on Madison Street.

"So are the Yankees," Ben replied without turning his head. "Just be quiet and trust me."

It was lunch time, and few civilians were about. No one seemed to pay them any heed as they passed. A few local girls and a handful of camp-followers from parts unknown rode out with federals, and the few soldiers who saw them looked enviously at the young man on horseback and his pretty passenger. Had they paid more attention, they might have noticed that Ben's uniform missed a few of its accessories and wondered why he rode bareheaded. But no one stopped them, and soon they had skirted the downtown area and headed east toward Monte Sano Mountain.

"How did you get through the pickets?" Lucinda asked when they had safely passed the last house.

"Now that I know where they are, I can avoid them," he replied. "Keep your head down and hold on tight. We're going up the mountain."

Lucinda did as she was told, and Ben left the road to follow a creek bed straight up Monte Sano. The terrain was rough, and often Ben called to her to duck as they passed under low-hanging tree branches. The horse stumbled several times on loose rocks and outcropping roots, but kept moving steadily up.

It seemed to Lucinda that they had been going straight up long enough to have reached heaven itself before Ben finally stopped to let the horse rest and drink from the stream. Her arms ached from hanging on, and her dress—a pale green print she had put on fresh for her hoped-for release—was badly snagged.

"We're almost to the crest," Ben told her. They would have to cross the toll road that bisected the mountain, then Lucinda knew they'd have to go down as steep a grade as they had come up. She didn't see how it could be done; surely the horse would fall and send them both plunging down the steep mountainside.

As if reading her thoughts, Ben explained his plan.

"We'll work parallel to the road and switch back and forth until we get past the steepest part."

"Where are we going?" she asked.

"To our main camp for now. Tomorrow I'll take you on to Highmeadows."

Lucinda was about to ask Ben how far the camp was, but he spurred the horse, and she had to give her full attention to keeping her seat and attempting to dodge as many branches as she could. At the edge of the toll road, Ben stopped and listened for tell-tale hoofbeats. Hearing none, he walked the horse across the road and into the thick underbrush on the other side. The process of going downhill by switching back and forth was tedious and took much longer than the ascent. When at last they reached the foot of the mountain, Ben stopped and dismounted.

"Time to rest," he said, and lifted Lucinda down. With a tender hand he brushed away a few twigs that had tangled in her hair.

"You were the last person I expected to see come through that door," she said. "Where on earth did you get that federal uniform?"

He smiled. "One of our prisoners kindly loaned it to me."

"Prisoners?" she repeated. "At Highmeadows?"

"No, of course not. Some federals came too close to the guerrilla camp and we were able to capture them."

"Ben, why did you do this? You know you could hang for wearing a Yankee uniform."

"They'll have to catch me first." He reached for Lucinda's hand and pressed it to his lips, then continued to hold it loosely. "When Mrs. Sherrill told me you'd been arrested, I had to come after you."

"But my arrest had nothing to do with you, and I'd probably have been let go in a day or so, anyway."

"Maybe, and maybe not. Anyway, aren't you even a *little* bit glad to see me?"

"I'm not sure," Lucinda replied truthfully. "I'm still trying to figure out what happens now."

"That's easy. Next we ride through the Paint Rock Valley to the camp. And that means it's time for me to get rid of this blue uniform."

Ben reached into his saddlebag and pulled out a light-colored shirt and homespun trousers. "I'll be back in a minute." He walked off into the woods and reappeared moments later, looking like an ordinary dirt farmer. "Now I'll just be hanged as a bushwhacker," he said cheerfully.

"You don't seem very concerned," Lucinda said as he helped her back on the horse.

"Well, we've been patrolling for a good six weeks, and in all that time we've been chased by a lot of Yankees, but our prisoners are the only ones that have come anywhere near the main camp."

"How have all of you been living?" Lucinda asked, knowing that the small amounts of food supplied by—or taken from—her aunt wouldn't feed very many fighting men.

"Different ways. Off the land, mostly. One of the federal trains we stopped carried gold, and that'll keep us going a long time if we can just get somewhere to use it."

"How will you do that?"

Ben turned in the saddle and smiled back at Lucinda. "I hope you and Mrs. Sherrill can help us."

"I can't go back to Huntsville," Lucinda said, acknowledging the sad truth.

"There are other towns. Once we cross the Tennessee River we'll be in Confederate territory. For the present, Mrs. Sherrill will be glad you're out of the Yankee's clutches."

"Did she know you were going to do this?" Lucinda asked, but Ben merely laughed and shook his head.

"I think you'd better just be quiet and hang on. The way's getting a bit steep."

Lucinda didn't try to answer him. Her head had begun to pound and her mind churned with questions, none of which had answers.

Nothing Ben had told her prepared Lucinda for the sight of the guerrilla camp. It was so well-hidden that Lucinda would have passed right by the entrance and never noticed it. Ben lifted her from the saddle and led the horse into dense underbrush. "We'll have to walk in," he explained.

Several hundred yards farther a guard in a tattered Confederate uniform called out a challenge, then recog-

nized Ben and waved them on. Presently they came to a
gap in the woods, and before them, in a lush valley bisected
by a creek, Lucinda saw several dozen dwellings, ranging
from tents to roughly-built cabins. Men were coming and
going, some tending livestock, others cleaning rifles and
carrying boxes of ammunition.

"How do you like it?" Ben asked, obviously proud of the
guerrillas' makeshift headquarters.

"It's certainly big," Lucinda said.

"You haven't seen the best part yet," Ben said proudly.
"See that shed over there? That's our special barracks."

Lucinda looked in the direction Ben pointed and saw a
small building guarded by several armed men. "What is
it?" she asked.

"That's where we keep the Yankees that got too curious."

"I had no idea all of this was here," she said faintly.

"Neither do the Yankees," Ben said with satisfaction.
"Now come along and meet the woman who cooks for us.
You can stay in her tent tonight."

The Widow Jackson greeted Lucinda warmly with a
smile that showed she had long since lost most of her teeth.

"I don't get much female company," she said, folding a
blanket to make a seat for Lucinda.

"How did you happen to come here?" Lucinda asked.
She thought it was a strange place for a lone woman.

"Well, the Yankees burned me out, you know," she said
in a matter-of-fact tone. "They'd already killed my oldest
boy and run the others off. Word got around and I was sent
for, and I been here ever since."

"Don't you have anywhere else to go?"

"Oh, yes, Missy. I got a sister in Stevenson, and I'll head

that way one o' these days. But right now, I figure this is as close as I'll get to fightin' Yankees. These boys need me, and they treat me like their ma. Sometimes they comes in hurt, and I take care of them. There's plenty for you to do, if you've a mind to stay," she added, looking speculatively at Lucinda.

"I'm going on to my aunt's," Lucinda replied. "I don't know how to do much, anyway," she added, admiring the expert way the older woman had been preparing the evening meal while talking to her.

"Well, it's probably for the good," the widow said, throwing some potatoes into an iron pot. "You're too purty—all the fellows'd be too busy fightin' over you to worry about the Yankees."

"I doubt it," Lucinda said, smiling in spite of herself.

"Is that your man what brung you in?"

Lucinda shook her head. "Ben's not my beau," she said. The word reminded her of Alice Ann's complaint that neither of them had any beaux. *How long ago that seems now,* Lucinda thought. Yet it had been only a few months.

"More's the pity," the widow said. "A purty little thing like you ought to have a man looking out for her."

Ben came back to have supper with Lucinda but didn't stay to talk, saying he had to confer with "the captain." Lucinda wrapped herself in a blanket, lay down on the ground in Mrs. Jackson's tent, and tried to sort out the day's tumultuous events. She wondered what had happened in Huntsville when she was missed. Viola would have been bringing her dinner shortly after Ben whisked her away, but even before that the guard would probably have come to his senses and sounded the alarm.

Had they pursued her? Surely Seth Russell would know

she would go to Highmeadows. If he came there looking for her, what would he do if he found her? *This is all Ben's fault,* she told herself, allowing a small flicker of anger to kindle itself. That he had done it for her, perhaps because he wrongly thought that she had been imprisoned on his account, made it even worse. And perhaps worst of all was her knowledge that she neither wanted nor could return Ben's love.

Lucinda shivered and pulled the blanket more tightly around her body. After a long while, she slept.

"Major?"

Seth opened his eyes, seeing nothing in the darkness. "Yes?"

"You reckon the Rebs is gonna shoot us?" one of his men asked.

"No, Corporal. If they were going to do that, we'd already be dead."

"Mebbe so. But I think we'd better say us some prayers, anyhow."

"We'd better get some sleep, too. Goodnight, Corporal."

Long after the others had fallen asleep, Seth stared into the darkness, thinking of the times he had watched Lucinda in prayer. *There must be a knack to it,* he thought, wishing he knew what it was.

"Wake up, missy," a voice at her elbow said. "Your young man said you was to have your breakfast now."

Lucinda struggled to a sitting position and looked about, surprised that she had slept through the early morning noises of the camp. The food—coffee made from parched acorns and the ever-present corn mush—was simple but filling. The Widow Jackson gave each man a hardtack biscuit and a pull of beef jerky. That, along with the abundant wild berries, nuts, and edible grasses, would provide them an adequate lunch. For supper, the widow cooked whatever the men brought in.

"We got a calf last month," she said, "and we're fattenin' a couple o' hogs. We get lots o' rabbits and squirrels, of course, and venison ever' now and then. They bring in chickens and eggs real regular, too."

Lucinda knew about the two hogs, the eggs, and chickens, and she wondered what else Highmeadows might unwittingly have supplied to the camp larder.

"What about the Yankees?" Lucinda asked, pointing in the direction of their compound. "Who feeds them?"

"They gets what the rest does, after we've done eatin'. We take good care o' them. They're our fire insurance."

"Fire insurance?" Lucinda echoed.

"I guess you ain't heard the story in Huntsville, since you been in jail and all," the widow said, warming to her subject. "General Mitchel's been sendin' out night patrols, tryin' to find this camp. One by one they've been ambushed, a few o' the Yankees shot, some gettin' away, the rest brought here.

"Two days ago we heard that the general was goin' to burn every house in the county and was sendin' a patrol out to do it. Well, our boys met 'em under a flag of truce and Cap'n Gurley told the Yankees to tell the general that we had about fifty Yankee prisoners. Every time they burned a house, we'd hang one o' their men."

"Oh!" Lucinda exclaimed. "Did it work?"

The widow laughed. "You don't smell no smoke, do

you?"

"Lucinda!"

Ben stood by the tent, holding the reins of two horses. "We'd better get started," he said.

"Thank you for your hospitality," Lucinda said to the widow.

"You're welcome, Missy. Come back an' see us again, hear?"

"These are Yankee horses," Ben said, boosting Lucinda onto the saddle of a roan. "I'm afraid this is the smallest one I could find." He mounted a larger black horse, which pranced sideways and tossed his head as if he knew Ben wasn't his master.

Ben had left a pair of trousers for her the night before, and as she straddled the horse's back, Lucinda knew she must make a strange appearance. Her skirts bunched up around her waist and billowed out behind her in strange contrast to the too-large pants that covered her legs. *Viola would have a hissey fit if she saw me now,* Lucinda thought. But the trousers would make it easier for her to ride in the strange McClellan saddle.

Morning mist still shrouded the tops of the hills as they rode out of the valley, surrounded by the sounds of summer.

"It's hard to believe that this area could be a battleground," Lucinda observed, her gesture taking in the beauty around them.

"Unfortunately it is. We'll have to stay in the woods as long as we can, or we might find ourselves part of a skirmish."

"Do you really think it's wise for me go Highmeadows?" Lucinda asked after they had ridden for some time in silence. "Surely the federals would look for me there first off."

"Well," Ben replied, "that's presuming they have the time and inclination to come after you in the first place. With all that General Mitchel has to worry about, I can't believe that capturing you would be that important."

"There's one federal officer who might look for me. He let us stay in our house and he's kept Papa from being arrested. For my aunt's safety, I'd have to give myself up if he finds me."

"That would be foolish. Don't make me put that blue uniform on again—it might not work so well a second time."

"I'm not so sure it worked that well this time," Lucinda replied.

"We'll see," Ben said, and then fell silent as they entered a flat, open plateau. "This is the most dangerous section."

At almost the same moment, they heard horses approaching at a fast pace from the south. Without waiting to see who they were, Ben urged his horse into a gallop and headed for the nearest cover. Lucinda followed suit, but her mount seemed reluctant to go faster than a sedate canter. When she lashed the gelding's withers with the reins, he broke gait. Ben had already reached the edge of the woods when he looked back and saw her horse rearing. Instantly he rode back to Lucinda and seized her horse's bridle. "Hang on!" Ben cried and galloped on, pulling her horse after him.

The delay had been brief but costly. Before they could reach the shelter of the woods, several blue-clad horsemen rode into view, and Lucinda's heart sank. She didn't want to go south with Ben, but neither did she want to be taken prisoner again.

"They've seen us." Ben handed Lucinda her reins and motioned ahead toward the west. "There's a stream just ahead," he said quickly. "Ride in it to cover your tracks. It'll lead you all the way to Highmeadows."

"What about you? What will you do?"

"Don't worry. I know a thing or two about dodging patrols. Now ride!"

Lucinda did as she was told, fervently hoping that her Yankee horse would behave. Ahead she saw the stream that Ben had mentioned. A few more yards and she would be there.

"Halt!" A voice behind her cried, and Lucinda turned to see two of the blue-clad soldiers only a few feet away. One pointed a bayoneted rifle at her and looked as if he wouldn't mind using it.

Lucinda reined in her horse, which promptly began to rear and sidestep again.

The man with the rifle seized the bridle and looked at the animal with interest. "Say, where'd you get this horse?" he asked.

"A friend loaned it to me," Lucinda replied.

"I'll bet!" the man growled. "This here's a federal saddle. Where's the man that it belongs to?"

"I don't know," Lucinda replied.

She turned as two more soldiers in blue joined them, flanking Ben.

"We got the girl," her captor said.

The older man smiled in triumph. "We caught this Rebel. And he's riding Major Russell's horse."

nine

Numb with shock, Lucinda reeled in the saddle almost as if she had been struck. She had thought that Ben's horse looked vaguely familiar, and now she knew why. Had she paid more attention to the major's horse and less to the man who rode it, she would have recognized the black stallion immediately. How stupid she had been!

I must have slept near him last night, she realized. Now she knew why he hadn't visited her prison room lately, knowledge that brought no comfort.

"Come along," the soldier with the rifle said. He took the reins from Lucinda and turned back toward the clearing, leading her horse.

On the trip into town, Ben and the soldier leading Star rode ahead. Ben's hands were tied behind his back. They rode in silence, having been warned not to attempt to communicate, and Lucinda wondered what Ben must be thinking. In freeing her—which he had certainly done bravely—he'd managed to get himself captured. Now Lucinda would be considered a fugitive, while Ben. . . .

Lucinda didn't want to think about how the federals might deal with him. At best, he would become a prisoner of war. At worst, if considered to be a spy, he would be executed. Ben had spoken of being hanged in joking terms, but Lucinda knew enough about the rules of war to know that hanging was a distinct possibility. The thought made her blood run cold. *God, help me to find some way to help*

156

him, she prayed.

The captives' arrival created quite a stir in the streets of Huntsville. Word of Lucinda's dramatic escape had spread through the town like wildfire. Now only a day later, here she was riding back in with Ben Bradley (who was supposed to be with the other Huntsville Rifles), and both in federal custody. For her part, Lucinda didn't mind being stared at. She only hoped that someone among the many gawkers would have the presence of mind to tell her father.

When the party arrived at General Mitchel's headquarters, a noisy debate broke out over which soldiers should have the honor of taking them inside. In the ensuing confusion Lucinda managed to speak to Ben.

"Is there a Yankee major named Russell at the camp?" she asked, and he nodded.

"Yes. I took his horse. Lucinda, I'm so sorry—" Ben began, but he was pulled from the saddle before he could finish.

The fact that Ben still seemed more concerned about her than himself made Lucinda feel even worse. If only he had left well enough alone! Inside headquarters, she had an unpleasant sense of deja vu as they were led into the room where she had been questioned prior to her imprisonment. They were immediately ushered into the library and told to wait without talking. She glanced at Ben with what she hoped was encouragement, but he looked even more grim.

In a moment, the general entered, accompanied by two armed soldiers. "Miss Matthews," he said, bowing slightly in her direction. "And who have we here?" he asked, turning to Ben.

"Benjamin Bradley, first lieutenant, Madison Rifles, Confederate States of America," he replied proudly.

"You are not in uniform, however," the General observed. "I must therefore assume that you are one of the notorious guerrillas."

Only faint color tinging his cheeks betrayed Ben's agitation. His voice was firm and clear as he spoke. "I'm a first lieutenant in the Madison Rifles, presently unable to get through federal lines to return to my unit."

"I suppose you have papers to prove it?" the General asked.

"Not with me," Ben answered.

The General turned to Lucinda. "Is this the man who took you from federal custody yesterday?"

Lucinda said nothing, and the general looked back at Ben. "A number of witnesses saw a fair-haired man in a blue uniform riding down Madison Street with a girl behind him about the time Miss Matthews's guard was rendered unconscious. Apparently you surprised the guard, then aided and abetted the escape of a federal prisoner. Isn't that so, Mr. Bradley?"

Ben glanced at Lucinda, then back at General Mitchel. "Yes, I rode into town and took Miss Matthews away. But she had no idea that I intended to free her. She went with me only because I forced her to do so."

General Mitchel looked from Lucinda to Ben. "In that case, it seems that a charge of kidnapping should be added to Mr. Bradley's crimes."

"He didn't kidnap me," Lucinda protested, but Ben interrupted her.

"General Mitchel, you should know that Miss Matthews and I are engaged to be married. When I learned she was being detained, my only thought was to free her. She's an entirely innocent party to my actions."

Oh, we're engaged, are we? Lucinda thought. She glanced at Ben in surprise, but he continued to look at the general.

"Very well, Mr. Bradley," General Mitchel replied. "You have defended the lady well enough. I'll talk with you later. Take him to the back room," the general directed one of the guards, "and return Miss Matthews to the house where she was before young Lochinvar here rode to her rescue."

At the general's last words Ben's face reddened, but to Lucinda's relief he said nothing more as he was led away. When the general turned to leave the room, Lucinda spoke quickly.

"Sir, I would like a word with you in private."

"I do not wish to discuss your detention," he said coolly.

"Nor do I. But I have some information I think you should know."

"Very well," the general said somewhat wearily, and with a wave of his hand he dismissed the other guard. "What is this important information, Miss Matthews?"

Lucinda took a deep breath and spoke earnestly, willing her voice to be strong. "I know where Major Russell is being held," she said.

The general's expression did not change. "I heard that your friend was riding his horse when you were captured. Have you actually seen the major, then?"

"No, sir. But I know where some federal soldiers are being held. I am certain that he is among them."

"And I suppose you're willing to tell me where he is in exchange for your freedom?"

"Not exactly." Lucinda's throat felt dry and she paused, silently praying for the right words. "I propose an exchange of Major Russell for Lieutenant Bradley."

"Impossible!" the General exclaimed. "He cannot be allowed to continue his guerrilla activities."

"Then let him return to his unit—see him safely across the Tennessee River, and I can promise you he won't bother you again."

"Without being punished for what he has done?" There was an edge of incredulity in the general's voice, but Lucinda persisted.

"Do you want Major Russell back? Or would you rather have him held as a permanent hostage?"

The general considered her question for a moment, then slowly nodded his head. "Yes, I'd like to have Major Russell back. He's the only decent aide I have. I might consider it if the exchange included the rest of the federal prisoners, as well."

"You know that can't be done," Lucinda said, not taking her eyes from his for a moment. "But perhaps I might manage two or three of the others."

"And just how do you propose to effect this plan?" the general asked. He sounded cautiously interested, and Lucinda spoke rapidly, hoping that what she was making up on the spur of the moment would make sense to him.

"Give me leave to go to the place where the major is being held. If the commander there approves, I'll come back and tell you. The exchange can be made outside the city under a flag of truce."

"And once you're out of town, what is to prevent you from escaping again?"

"My obligation to Lieutenant Bradley, for one thing," she replied. "You could take my father into custody until I return, as well. You also have my word as a Christian that all will go as I say it will."

The general was silent, his expression inscrutable. A look crossed his face that Lucinda had never seen on it—admiration, perhaps, or amusement—but it quickly faded, leaving him looking even sterner.

"If I should permit you to do this, you will still be in our custody," he said.

"I understand," Lucinda replied, her heart beginning to beat again. *He's going to agree to it,* she realized.

"I begin to see why Major Russell spoke so eloquently on your behalf," the general said with grudging admiration. "Against my better judgment, I'm going to allow you to try your scheme."

"Thank you, General Mitchel. You won't be sorry."

"There is one important condition, however," he warned. "Mr. Bradley must leave Huntsville immediately on Major Russell's release. If he is seen again, he will be hanged, no questions asked."

"I understand, and there is also one condition on which I must insist."

General Mitchel looked annoyed. "And just what is that?"

"You must promise that I won't be followed. If the guerrillas were to think that their security had been breached, I couldn't be responsible for what might happen to their prisoners—including Major Russell."

The general rubbed his chin and shook his head, muttering something under his breath that Lucinda couldn't hear. Aloud he said, "If this is to be done, it should be done immediately. Are you able to travel again so soon?"

Lucinda nodded. "Yes, but I'd like to ride my own horse."

"No. I don't want anyone else to know about this. I'll send for my daughter's saddle and mare. In the meantime, you can have some lunch." His glance took in her ruined dress and the too-long men's trousers hanging down from it, and for the first time Lucinda realized how strange she must look. "You can wear her riding habit as well," he added.

"All right," she agreed.

"An escort will take you past the pickets and wait until you return. After that, you're on your own."

Lucinda had tried to sound and appear perfectly confident, but as soon as the general left, she sank into a chair and closed her eyes. Her whole body trembled as she thought of what lay ahead for her. A great deal depended on how well she carried out her mission.

Let me do well, Lord, she prayed. For Ben and the major, she had to.

Although she had been assured that she wouldn't be followed, Lucinda kept glancing back uneasily after she left her escort at the picket outpost atop Chapman Mountain. To her relief, she saw no one. She hadn't dared to go to the camp the way Ben had done. It would be longer but safer to cross Chapman Mountain and work her way to the east, away from the main road, until she found the camp.

"Well, Jenny Lind," Lucinda said to the mare that the general had provided for her to ride, "I hope you're up to some cross-country riding."

The little animal tossed her head as if she understood. Until the Mitchel family's arrival, Jenny Lind had belonged to Virginia Clay, and just before Lucinda's detention, a friend of theirs had seen the general's daughter riding the mare and yelled at her to get off. That afternoon the girl's brother had been arrested, and so far as Lucinda knew, remained in custody. *The general is a hard man,* she had told Ben, and she knew it was true.

Lucinda left the road and headed in the direction of the camp. It was slow going through the thick undergrowth, and she could only hope that she was heading in the right direction. At length she found the dead oak tree that marked the trail Ben had taken, and as she approached the camp perimeter, Lucinda heard a rustling in the brush. A bearded man garbed in a Confederate uniform that had seen better days emerged, his rifle pointed and at the ready.

"Who goes there?"

"Lucinda Matthews, from Huntsville. I was here yesterday with Lieutenant Bradley."

"Oh, yes, Miss Matthews." The guard lowered his rifle and looked past her. "Where's the lieutenant?"

"I'm alone today. Can you take me to Captain Gurley?"

"Sure, ma'am. Come this way—but you'll have to lead your horse."

Everything seemed exactly as it had the day before. Lucinda glanced at the windowless building where the federal prisoners were being kept. If only she could bring Major Russell out and go! But she knew that gaining his freedom wouldn't be that simple.

"Well, Miss Matthews, this is an unexpected pleasure," Captain Gurley greeted her. "Please be seated," he added, moving some tack from an upended barrel that served as a makeshift chair. "I'll have some refreshment brought right away. You look like you can use it."

Lucinda accepted a dipper of spring water but declined the offered hardtack. "Thank you," she said when she had slaked her thirst. "I'm afraid you won't like what I have to tell you." Quickly Lucinda sketched the events that had preceded her visit.

Captain Gurley heard her out, then asked her to repeat the story, almost as if he doubted that Lucinda could be telling him the truth. He strode around the tent, his hands clasped behind his back, his expression dour.

"Major Russell is the highest-ranking prisoner we could hope to capture," he said at last. "I'm not inclined to let him go."

"Then Lieutenant Bradley's life could be the forfeit," Lucinda said flatly. "Does keeping the major mean that much to you?"

A muscle worked in the captain's jaw, but instead of answering her question, he asked one of his own. "Was Lieutenant Bradley wearing a federal uniform when he was captured?"

"No, but he was when he rode into Huntsville, and he was seen by a number of people. If General Mitchel wasn't so eager to have his adjutant back, Ben would probably already have been formally charged with spying."

Captain Gurley sighed and rubbed the back of his neck. "You're a brave young lady," he said at last. "I wonder if Lieutenant Bradley has any idea how lucky he is to have an advocate like you."

"He doesn't know anything about this. I wasn't allowed to tell anyone I was coming here."

"How do I know you weren't followed?" the captain asked. He looked up at the surrounding hills as if he expected to see blue uniforms issue from them at any moment.

"I came the long way around and rode mostly in the

woods. I'd know if anyone had followed me."

"I believe you would, at that," Captain Gurley said, allowing himself a faint smile.

"What shall I tell the general?" Lucinda prompted. "I must report back to him immediately."

Captain Gurley shrugged and spread his hands in a gesture of helplessness. "For Lieutenant Bradley's sake I suppose I'll have to go along, although it galls me to let General Mitchel have anything he wants. Tell him I'll have the major and two men of his choice waiting tomorrow at noon at the top of Chapman Mountain. But if the general tries anything, Major Russell is a dead man."

The guerrilla commander's matter-of-fact words chilled Lucinda. She knew that this man meant what he said. "Thank you, Captain Gurley. You may have saved Ben's life."

"I hope so, ma'am. Can you find your way back alone?"

"I'm sure I can. And I'll make certain that no one sees that I came from this direction."

"Until tomorrow, then. Good luck, Miss Matthews."

Lucinda took the reins of Virginia Clay's horse and left the camp quickly, with another brief glance at the place where the guerrillas' prisoners were being held.

You won't have to stay there much longer, Major Russell, Lucinda thought. She wished she could see him, but she knew that was out of the question. She had a job to finish.

Lucinda was ushered into the general's presence as soon as she returned. Her brief report seemed to satisfy him, but he was still skeptical that the proposed exchange would actually work.

"I know these Rebels and their tricks," he said darkly.

"And I know that Captain Gurley will keep his word," Lucinda countered. "If your men go anywhere near the area while Major Russell and the others are being brought out, they will be shot."

"So I understand," the general said. "I can assure you that it would go very ill with everyone in Huntsville should that happen." He dropped his riveting glance from Lucinda, who hadn't flinched under it, and called to the guard at the door. "Sergeant, see Miss Matthews back to her detention quarters."

He could at least have thanked me for my trouble, Lucinda thought, almost too tired to work up any righteous indignation.

"Let's go, Missy," the sergeant said as he took her arm with mock courtesy. She tried to pull away, but he held her even more tightly.

Outside headquarters, Lucinda tried to look back toward her house, but her guard urged her on. She walked down Adams Street beside him, aware that a casual observer might mistake them for a federal soldier and his sweetheart, out for a pleasant stroll.

They turned onto Randolph Street and soon reached the house which she had so recently fled. A different sergeant now guarded the door, an older man who barely glanced up as Lucinda was escorted to the second-floor room she had hoped never to see again.

As the key turned in the lock, Lucinda looked around the room. It seemed impossible that she had been away only a single night, considering all that had happened in the meantime. She lay down on the cot but didn't try to sleep. Her mind kept going over the exchange that was to take place the next day.

It's got to work, she prayed. She didn't want to think about what might happen to Ben and the major if it didn't. Lucinda didn't fear for her own safety—she knew that whatever else might happen, the general would have to let her go sooner or later—but she wasn't so sure about what might happen to the three men at the center of her life.

To her sorrow, Lucinda acknowledged that her arrest had made keeping her father out of a northern prison more difficult. At best it was unlikely that he'd be allowed to continue his unofficial attempts to ease the burden of the occupation.

Then there was Ben. Because of her, he was in great danger. Not only did Lucinda want him out of federal custody; he must also be allowed to return to the Confederate lines. The information he now had could help end the occupation. But primarily, Lucinda wanted to make certain that he didn't suffer further on her account. If he really loved her—and it seemed that he thought he did, at least— he would be hurt that she didn't return his love.

Lucinda hesitated to give words to the way she felt about Major Russell. Her feelings for him, from active dislike to grudging attraction, had changed so gradually that she couldn't name their beginnings or foresee their end. At the moment, her main concern was that he must be returned to Huntsville so Ben could go free. After that. . . . Lucinda tried to envision her own future and could not.

Lean not unto thine own understanding, she reminded herself, and felt somewhat comforted.

Just after dawn, the guard unlocked the door, waking her. "General Mitchel wants to see you," he said.

"Is he letting me go?" she asked as the sergeant led her

down the stairs and put her into a carriage.

"All I know is he wants to see you," he replied, getting in beside her for the brief ride to headquarters.

The general looked up from some papers when she entered. He made no effort to stand, nor did he offer her a chair. He seemed somewhat preoccupied, and at first Lucinda feared that he had changed his mind.

"I"ve given some thought to this exchange. Since it was your idea, I want you to take part in it. Perhaps your presence will help to keep the transaction honest."

Afraid that he might change his mind if he knew how much she wanted to go, Lucinda tried not to look pleased. It would be much better to see what was happening first hand than to be back in her locked room worrying about it.

"I think both men are honorable. There shouldn't be any trouble," she said.

"I hope you're right. Captain Warren and Sergeant Wise will ride with you. Lieutenant Bradley will be escorted to the Tennessee River as soon as the exchange is completed. From there, he'll be on his own. My men have orders to shoot to kill if he does anything amiss. For your sake, I hope he'll behave himself."

"I am sure that he will," Lucinda murmured.

"Perhaps it would help if you told him that yourself," the general said. "Guard, bring the prisoner in," he called to awaiting soldier, and almost immediately Ben was led in, his hands tied behind his back. He looked as if he hadn't slept, but his face brightened when he saw Lucinda.

"Have they let you go?" he asked.

"Not yet," she said.

"Bring the prisoner out directly," General Mitchel said

as he walked toward the door. "The others will be waiting."

From half the length of the room, Ben and Lucinda looked at one another. Ben spoke first.

"I've just been told that I'm to be exchanged for a federal officer. Did you know that?"

"Yes, I heard. The general has agreed to let you go if he gets his adjutant and two other soldiers in return."

"I always did think a Confederate was worth three Yankees. I'm happy to see that the federals agree," he said, attempting a smile.

The guard pulled roughly at Ben's sleeve in warning at that remark and shook his head.

"Oh, Lucinda, I'm sorry I made such a mess of things for you."

"Don't say that," Lucinda said gently, pained by the hurt in his voice. "I know you did what you thought was best."

"But nothing has turned out the way I intended it to."

"It's not your fault. Forget it, as I already have."

"And will you forget me too?" His expression was so wistful that Lucinda felt her heart twist. She took a step forward, but her guard laid a restraining hand on her arm.

"You know I could never forget you, no matter what," Lucinda said, meaning every word. It was no lie to say that she'd always remember him. And after all he had risked for her, Lucinda couldn't tell him that she didn't love him.

"I wish we were married," he began, his voice thick.

"Hush!" Lucinda cried. "Wish instead for the war to end soon."

The guards had been listening avidly to their conversation, but now they exchanged glances and nodded. "Time to go," Ben's guard said.

"Goodbye, Lucinda. Keep safe." Ben mustered a ragged half-smile.

"You, too," she said. Then, turning back for one last look, Ben was gone. It was almost enough to make Lucinda wish she could love Ben. Almost, but not quite.

"Come along, Missy," Lucinda's guard directed, and she walked out of the room with her head held high. Mutely she accepted a hand up to her mount and tried to focus her attention on the important matter at hand, as she had advised Ben to do.

Lucinda looked up and down Adams Street but saw no civilians. It was Sunday, and while most of their neighbors would be in church at that hour, she doubted that her father was among them. She wondered briefly what he'd done when he found out she was gone and wished she could tell him she was all right.

Lucinda rode between Captain Warren and her guard. Well behind them, Ben followed, flanked by two guards. Each of the three guards led a horse for the released federal soldiers.

The day was pleasantly warm, and the sun was near its zenith when the party reached the agreed rendezvous east of Huntsville. Nervously, Lucinda scanned the empty road before them. They halted, and for a moment the only sounds were the impatient stamping of the horses and the rattle of tack as their mounts tossed their heads.

"Are you certain this is the right place?" Captain Warren asked Lucinda, his tone almost accusing.

"Yes," Lucinda replied. At the same moment, Major Russell's horse, led by her guard, neighed and pranced sideways in an attempt to pull free. Lucinda glanced over at the horse, and when she looked back at the road, she saw several horsemen approaching.

"I make out three blue uniforms and three others with a white flag," Captain Warren said, lowering his field glass. "All hold your positions until they are within hailing distance. I'll be spokesman."

Lucinda shaded her eyes and strained to see the men riding toward them. As the captain had reported, there were three men in blue, but Lucinda had eyes for only one. She knew which was Major Russell, all right, and she watched intently as he rode ever nearer.

"Hold our truce flag high, Sergeant. I want no excuse for any guerrilla tricks."

Captain Gurley also lifted his white flag and waved it as the party grew near.

"Halt!" Captain Warren shouted when they were perhaps fifty yards distant. "That's close enough! Is that you, Major Russell?"

"It is," he called back. "I have Corporal Watkins and Sergeant Pierce with me. Both men are slightly wounded."

"Lieutenant Bradley?" Captain Gurley called out, although Lucinda knew that by now Ben's blond hair and beard would have confirmed his identity.

"Yes, sir!" Ben answered in a firm voice.

"Very well," Captain Warren said. "Untie his hands, Corporal. Miss Matthews, you and the Lieutenant are to walk out to meet the major and his party halfway. Stay in the middle of the road until each man has reached his own side. Do you understand?"

"Yes, sir," Lucinda replied, sliding down from her horse without waiting for anyone to help her. Ben walked beside her, rubbing his chafed wrists. All was quiet as they slowly made their way to the exchange point. Lucinda fixed her eyes on Major Russell, who was looking from her to Ben as if he doubted what he saw.

"Miss Matthews, step forward until you are midway between the major and the lieutenant," Captain Warren called.

Lucinda turned to Ben and lightly touched his hand. "Goodbye. May God go with you."

Ben might have spoken, but Lucinda had already started walking away. She had covered only a few yards when Captain Warren called for her to hold her position.

"Gentlemen, come forward."

The men to be exchanged began to walk toward Lucinda, and as they drew closer, Seth confirmed his first impression, that the Rebel was the same man who had fired at and captured him.

How on earth did Lucinda get involved in this? he wondered as they met on either side of her and continued walking toward their respective sides.

Lucinda turned slightly so she could see all parties to the exchange. Major Russell's group, slowed by a limping man, took longer, but at last they, too, had reached their goal.

"Goodbye, Rebs!" Captain Warren called.

"We'll see you in battle!" Captain Gurley responded. His party galloped away in a cloud of red dust while Ben mounted the horse that Major Russell had ridden to the rendezvous and joined the two guards who would escort him to the Tennessee River.

Lucinda waved as they rode past and watched until they were out of sight. When she turned back, Lucinda saw Major Russell walking toward her. Although his face was covered with a stubbly dark beard and his hair was uncombed, to Lucinda he had never looked better.

"You were the last person I expected to see in the midst of a prisoner exchange," he said by way of greeting.

Lucinda longed to throw her arms around him and tell him how glad she was to see him. Instead, she stood mute as a statue, with legs that had turned to jelly and a pounding heart.

Seeing her stricken look and totally misreading the cause, Seth took her elbow and walked with her back to her horse. "You look exhausted. Come, I'll help you mount."

"Here's your horse, Major," Captain Warren said. "The guerrilla was riding it when we caught him. We'd better get away from here in case they decide to come after us."

"I don't think there's any danger now," Seth replied, but he left Lucinda, patted Star's flanks, and swung into the saddle, riding beside the captain with Lucinda and her guard just behind them.

"I never thought the exchange would come off," Captain Warren admitted as they rode along. Glancing back at Lucinda, he added, "I had no idea that a Rebel Miss could be so valuable."

"So valuable that I must be kept locked up!" Lucinda replied.

"I wish someone would tell me what's going on," Seth put in before the captain could answer Lucinda. "What did Miss Matthews have to do with this?"

"The whole thing was her idea. She even talked the guerrillas into giving us a three-for-one swap."

Puzzled, Seth turned to look at Lucinda. "How did you manage that?"

Briefly Lucinda told the story, trying to be fair to Ben but making it clear that escaping hadn't been her idea.

"When I realized that Lieutenant Bradley had your horse, I knew the guerrillas must have captured you. From there it was logical to think of arranging an exchange, and General Mitchel agreed to the plan."

"How extraordinary!" Seth said, looking at her with frank admiration.

"That's all well and good," Captain Warren said, "but Miss Matthews remains in custody."

Not if I have anything to say about it, Seth thought.

When they turned into Adams Street, he spoke to Captain Warren. "Take the wounded men to a surgeon immediately. Miss Matthews and I are going to see General Mitchel."

Private O'Brien saw them coming up the walk and hastened out to greet Seth. "It sure is good to have you back, sir."

"Thank you. Is General Mitchel here?"

"I believe he went somewhere with his daughter. He ought to be back soon."

"Tell the general I'm waiting for him in the library."

When they reached the room, Seth closed the door and motioned for Lucinda to be seated. "The past few days must have been a terrible ordeal," he said.

I suppose I must really look awful, Lucinda thought. Her borrowed riding habit was too large, making her look even more petite. She sat somewhat stiffly on the edge of a straight chair, and Seth pulled another up and sat facing her.

"I'm all right. I'm sure the past few days haven't been easy for you, either. How did you happened to be captured?"

"We were ambushed while trying to locate the guerrillas' main camp. They blindfolded us and locked us up in a dark shed at the camp. It seemed we were there for weeks instead of days."

"So now you have been a prisoner, too," Linda said, risking a slightly ironic smile.

His dark eyes held hers. "Yes, but I'm afraid I didn't handle it very well. I kept thinking of how calm you seemed, locked in that room. Tell me your secret, Miss Lucinda."

Lucinda half-smiled. "It's no secret, Major. As a child I gave my heart to Christ, and I trust Him to guide and protect me."

Seth looked dubious. "There must be more to it than that."

"It's hard to explain, but when I pray, the Holy Spirit gives me peace. That's really all there is to it."

"That's hard to believe."

"Maybe that's why the Bible calls it 'the peace that passeth all understanding.' If you were a Christian, you'd know it too."

Seth frowned. "I'm not really a bad person, though. I've always believed in God as Creator."

"Well, that's a start," Lucinda began, but she stopped speaking as General Mitchel entered. As Seth rose to greet him, the general broke into a rare smile and grasped his adjutant's hand.

"Welcome back, Major. I trust the exchange went well?"

"Yes, sir, thanks to Miss Matthews."

"And to her Rebel," the General put in. "If he hadn't decided to come after his sweetheart, you'd still be locked up."

Lucinda winced at the general's words. *He's not my sweetheart,* she wanted to say, but Major Russell hadn't seemed to notice.

"Miss Matthews is hardly a dangerous criminal. Surely keeping her in custody can serve no useful purpose."

"You forget our responsibility to keep these civilians in line. The impertinence and disrespect we receive from these people knows no bounds. Even the children—while you were away, two little girls put Rebel flags on their hoops, then flipped their skirts as our soldiers passed. I gave them a talking-to and sent them home, but that's the sort of attitude we must not permit. A line has to be drawn somewhere if we are to keep order."

"I know it isn't easy," Major Russell replied, suppressing a smile at the story. "But in return for her services to us, I'd like to ask that Miss Matthews be placed on probation. I will personally vouch for her behavior," he added. Seth glanced at Lucinda to gauge her reaction, but she sat staring at the floor, her hands demurely folded in her lap.

General Mitchel began pacing the room with his hands crossed behind his back. "Women!" he muttered. "A soldier shouldn't be bothered with them."

"Releasing Miss Matthews as a gesture of good will might work to ease some of the ill feeling against us."

The general stopped pacing and looked directly at Lucinda. "Once again the major has taken your part," he said. "I can't let you go unless I have your word that you won't seek to harm anyone in my command. Then you would remain on probation."

"Sir, I can assure you I never sought to harm anyone, nor will I in the future," Lucinda said earnestly. "I'm no different in that respect now than I was when you had me locked up the first time."

General Mitchel sighed and waved his hand. "For your impertinence you deserve to go back to your locked room, but for the major's sake, I'll release you. However, if you're brought before me again—"

"She won't be," Seth interrupted before the General could name a punishment great enough.

General Mitchel waved his hand in dismissal. "Go on, then. Major, I'll want you in my office as soon as you've made yourself presentable."

Seth took Lucinda's arm and walked with her to her home, drawing curious stares from passers-by.

"It seems that I am in your debt, Major," Lucinda said.

They had reached her front door, and Seth turned to face Lucinda. "No more than I am in yours. You did a brave thing, and I thank you for it. But there is something you could do for me."

What on earth could that be? Lucinda thought. "Yes, Major?"

"You could tell me more about being a Christian," he said.

Looking into his eyes, Lucinda saw that he was serious. "Then start by coming to church Sunday. You may sit with Papa and me, if you like," she added, seeing his hesitation.

"Despite what people would say about you?"

"God's house ought to be a place where all can be brothers."

"Your lieutenant is a lucky man," the major said. "I will try my best to be there Sunday. Good day, Miss Lucinda."

As he turned and walked away, Lucinda's heart sank. She wanted to call him back and tell him that Ben had no hold on her heart, but she knew she shouldn't. He had asked her for spiritual guidance, not for a declaration of love.

Seth Russell held her heart—and he didn't even know it.

ten

The next few days passed slowly for Lucinda. She enjoyed being able to sleep in her own house, a luxury she would never again take for granted, but she was disappointed not to see Major Russell. When she asked her father if he had seen him, he shook his head.

"Something's in the wind," he told her, but he didn't know exactly what.

The general's staff seemed preoccupied, lacking the time or inclination to speak to civilians. When Sunday finally arrived, Lucinda wondered if Major Russell would come to church. Perhaps his apparent desire to know more about her religion had been a passing fancy that he would never pursue. Still, Lucinda wore her best dress, full-skirted white lawn, lavishly embroidered with delicate pink roses.

I'm not really trying to impress him, she told herself, knowing otherwise.

Seth Russell stood before a full-length mirror in his room and surveyed his reflection. He scarcely recognized the man in the white planter's suit, ruffled shirt, and stringed tie who looked back at him. Frank Allison was not quite as broad-shouldered as Seth, so that the jacket pulled across the shoulders, but otherwise it was a good fit.

"Are you really going out in *that*?" Lieutenant Stryker asked as Seth passed him in the hall.

"Yes, I am. Good day." Seth enjoyed the lieutenant's astonishment, but his pleasure was brief as he realized that his first attempt to dress like the locals would probably also be his last.

That didn't matter, of course, but something—or someone else—did, and although Seth had tried to keep from thinking about Lucinda during the last few busy days, he hadn't succeeded. A clean break would be best, but Lucinda's invitation to join her at church had seemed so earnest that he knew he would have to go. After that. . . .

Unwilling to think past the present, Seth clamped on a broad-brimmed Panama hat and strode off down the street to church.

As they turned into Gates Street, Arnold spotted Seth standing at the edge of the churchyard.

"There's Major Russell, alone and out of uniform. I wonder why?"

"I invited him to sit with us. I hope you don't mind."

Her father gave her a searching glance. "I have no objection, but you should have told me."

"I wasn't sure he would come."

"Good day, Mr. Matthews, Miss Lucinda."

"Good day to you, Major." Arnold Matthews didn't offer to shake his hand, but gestured for Seth to accompany them inside.

As they entered the sanctuary, Lucinda covertly inspected the major's garb and wondered where he had gotten it. In his white suit, the handsome Yankee could pass for an Alabama planter. His change of clothing didn't fool anyone in the congregation, however. All knew that Lucinda had arranged to swap the major to save Ben

Bradley, and glances and whispers followed their progress down the aisle.

As the service began with the singing of the Doxology, Lucinda discovered that Seth Russell had a rich baritone voice. Her soprano was light but true, and their voices blended in perfect harmony. There was much about this man that she didn't know, Lucinda reflected, but she silently prayed for them both.

To Lucinda's disappointment, Pastor Ross was absent that day, and his replacement fumbled through a brief and uninspired sermon. If the major learned how to become a Christian, it certainly wouldn't be because of this service, she thought.

After the benediction, Arnold Matthews looked appraisingly at Seth. "You look almost human without your uniform, Major," he said.

Major Russell laughed. "Then perhaps you could call me Seth, rather than 'Major.'"

"Seth," Mr. Matthews repeated. "Adam and Eve's third son, if I remember correctly."

"Yes, born after Cain slew Abel." Then to Lucinda he added, "I'm at least that much of a biblical scholar, Miss Lucinda."

"I'm glad to hear it, sir," Lucinda said, and her father looked at them both as if he knew he had missed something, but wasn't sure what.

Reaching the corner where they would part, Seth told them he'd like to call on them that afternoon. "I have something to give you," he added.

"I wonder what the major could have for us," Lucinda said as she and her father continued on their way home.

"It'd be the first time a Yankee ever gave anyone around

here anything, that's certain!"

When Seth Russell arrived about two o'clock, back in his uniform and carrying an oddly-shaped parcel, Lucinda met him at the door. She was reminded of their first meeting, when he'd entered as an intruding enemy. He still wore union blue, but Lucinda had long since looked past that and come to love the man.

What did he feel for her?

Seth looked at Lucinda as if memorizing her features, and with equal boldness, she returned his gaze. Then her father joined them, breaking the spell.

"What do you have there?" he asked.

"Something I could be court-martialed for returning," Seth said, handing Mr. Matthews the package.

When she saw the contents, Lucinda gasped. "Henry's musket and the pistols you took from us!"

"I will have to trust you not to use them on our men," Seth said, looking directly at Lucinda.

"Thank you for doing this," Mr. Matthews said, obviously moved.

"It's no more than your due. I wanted you to have them before I left."

Lucinda put a hand to her throat at his words, but it was her father who asked Seth what he meant.

"General Mitchel has been recalled to Washington. We leave tomorrow morning."

"Will you be back?" Arnold asked.

Seth shrugged. "That remains to be seen. The general is to give an account of his actions, and he may or may not keep this command."

"And what about you? Does your fate hinge on the general's?" Lucinda asked, finally finding her voice.

"I am his adjutant. Where he goes, so do I."

Lucinda wondered if her face reflected her alarm. *I can't let him leave like this,* she thought, searching for a way to stop him and finding none.

"Well, Major, I can't say that Huntsville will be sorry to see your commander leave, but I wish you could stay."

Seth's eyes met Lucinda's again and she felt numb. "So do I. Miss Lucinda, I appreciate your interest in my spiritual welfare. I do intend to peruse the matter."

Seth turned back to Arnold, and wordlessly the men shook hands. He reached for Lucinda's hand and lightly pressed his lips against it.

"May God go with you," she managed to say.

"Thank you. I feel sure that He will."

Then he was gone, and Lucinda turned away, not wanting her father to read her emotions.

"I'm going to hide these weapons well," Arnold said. "We don't want to lose them a second time."

"The next Yankees may not be as kind as Major Russell," she managed to say, although her throat felt constricted and she was dangerously near tears.

As soon as her father had gone upstairs, Lucinda hurried out of the house, not even stopping for her bonnet, and half-ran to the Allison's house.

The front door was unguarded and unlocked, and Lucinda boldly entered, surprising a soldier who told her Major Russell's room was in the rear. *He's been staying in the old sewing room,* she realized as she reached the half-open door. She stopped, wondering what she could possibly say to him.

Seth stood by a dresser, putting clothing into a valise. When he looked up and saw Lucinda, his look of mingled surprise and joy told her that she needed no words. The few feet separating them were quickly bridged, and somehow she was in Seth's arms.

"You shouldn't be here," he said, tightening his embrace. "I know I ought to send you home, but I can't."

"And I can't let you leave thinking that I love Ben Bradley."

Seth relaxed his hold and pulled back, searching Lucinda's face.

"You don't?"

"I never have, really. Ben is just a special friend."

"Ah, sweet Lucinda. From the first moment I saw you, I knew I had let a Rebel girl conquer my heart. But when I met your brave Lieutenant Bradley, I thought that my love for you was hopeless."

"The Bible says that nothing is ever hopeless, Major."

He smiled down at her. "I don't plan to be in the army all my life. Please call me Seth."

"Seth," Lucinda repeated. "It's a beautiful name."

He pulled Lucinda to him again and his tender kiss told her the depth of his love for her. For a moment they stood quietly, content merely to be together. Then Seth released her and took a New Testament from his dresser.

"My mother gave me this when I left home, but I'll have to admit it hasn't seen much use. Will you help me find the hope you say is there?"

"Of course. But nobody else can accept Christ for you or on your behalf. It has to come from you."

"I know that. I suppose I was just waiting for someone to point me in the right direction—but I never would have expected it to be you!"

"God knows what He's doing," Lucinda said. "We just

have to trust Him to work things out."

Seth took both her hands in his and kissed her on the forehead. "Do you think you could ever marry a Yankee, Miss Matthews?"

Lucinda smiled tremulously and scarcely inclined her head. Seth picked her up and twirled her around until, giddy, she cried for him to put her down. He kissed her once more before speaking again.

"If that didn't mean 'yes,' please don't tell me."

"And if it did?"

"Then I thank God for it," he replied simply.

She came into his arms again, and they stood for a long moment, savoring their new love.

Their life together wouldn't be easy, Lucinda knew. But they wouldn't be alone. Lucinda thought of Paul's words and felt comforted.

It's true, she realized. Through Christ, she and Seth were more than conquerors.

author's notes

General Ormsby McKnight Mitchel left Huntsville on July 2, 1862, was subsequently promoted to brigadier general, and was reassigned to Hilton Head, South Carolina, where he died of yellow fever in October 1862.

General Don Carlos Buell was criticized for his conduct of the war. His command was transferred to General William Rosecarns, and Buell left the service in 1863.

Captain Frank Gurley survived the war to become sheriff of Madison County; the present town of Gurley, formerly Camden, was named for him.

Presbyterian minister Frederick Ross was arrested and detained for a time after praying that the Lord would, "bless our enemies and remove them from our midst as soon as seemeth good in Thy sight."

The federals evacuated Huntsville a month after General Mitchell went to Washington, returning in July of 1863 and remaining in control of the area for the rest of the war. Diaries and other records of the time provide a wealth of detail about the lives of ordinary citizens during the Civil War.

Today a visitor to Huntsville can walk down Adams Street and see the McDowell house, former federal headquarters, and dozens of other gracious antebellum homes. At the Huntsville Depot Museum, graffiti left by both federal and Confederate soldiers can be read on the walls.

The past is alive and well in the city of the Saturn moon rocket and the space shuttle.

A Letter To Our Readers

Dear Reader:

In order that we might better contribute to your reading enjoyment, we would appreciate your taking a few minutes to respond to the following questions. When completed, please return to the following:

Karen Carroll, Editor
Heartsong Presents
P.O. Box 719
Uhrichsville, Ohio 44683

1. Did you enjoy reading *More Than Conquerors*?
   ☐ Very much. I would like to see more books
      by this author!
   ☐ Moderately
      I would have enjoyed it more if _____

   _____

2. Are you a member of *Heartsong Presents*? Yes   No
   If no, where did you purchase this book? _____

   _____

3. What influenced your decision to purchase
   this book? (Circle those that apply.)

Cover	Back cover copy
Title	Friends
Publicity	Other _____

4. On a scale from 1 (poor) to 10 (superior), please rate the following elements.

    ___Heroine   ___Plot

    ___Hero   ___Inspirational theme

    ___Setting   ___Secondary characters

5. What settings would you like to see covered in *Heartsong Presents* books?

_____

_____

6. What are some inspirational themes you would like to see treated in future books?_____

_____

_____

7. Would you be interested in reading other *Heartsong Presents* titles?   Yes   No

8. Please circle your age range:

| Under 18 | 18-24 | 25-34 |
| 35-45 | 46-55 | Over 55 |

9. How many hours per week do you read? _____

Name _____

Occupation _____

Address _____

City _____ State _____ Zip _____

NEW! from Colleen L. Reece.

Lose yourself in the O'Donnell family saga as they capture the spirit of the American Dream

____**Veiled Joy**—For Joyous, her childhood is shattered when she is kidnapped and then abandoned. Never knowing her true identity, she grows up amid the California Gold Rush as the adopted daughter of Angus McFarlane, a lovable prospector.

Brit O'Donnell escapes the potato famine in Ireland to find a better life in Monterey, California. The Silver Rush will test the mettle of this determined young man.

The son of a Castilian patrician whose fortune was absconded, fifteen-year-old Carlos Montoya also ventures to California with dreams of silver.

Three seemingly separate lives, three undetermined destinies. . .to be brought together by the hand of God in the unforgiving California desert. HP43 BHSB-43 $2.95.

____**Tapestry of Tamar**—The world is a frightening place for Tamar O'Donnell. She escapes a marriage of convenience, only to find that again and again she must flee new dangers.

Living under a false name, she would like to accept the love and security offered by the young lawyer, Gordon Rhys, but she is afraid to trust him with the secret of her identity.

This time when she runs away she finds herself caught in a danger she cannot escape: the San Francisco earthquake of 1906. HP52 BHSB-52 $2.95.

REECE2

Heartsong

HEARTSONG PRESENTS TITLES AVAILABLE NOW:

(If ordering from this page, please remember to include it with the order form.)

HPS DECEMBER

·········Presents·········

Great Inspirational Romance at a Great Price!

Heartsong Presents books are inspirational romances in contemporary and historical settings, designed to give you an enjoyable, spirit-lifting reading experience. You can choose from 60 wonderfully written titles from some of today's best authors likeLauraine Snelling, Brenda Bancroft, Sara Mitchell, and many others.

When ordering quantities less than twelve, above titles are $2.95 each.

SEND TO: Heartsong Presents Reader's Service
  P.O. Box 719, Uhrichsville, Ohio 44683

Please send me the items checked above. I am enclosing $_____
(please add $1.00 to cover postage per order. OH add 6.5% tax. PA and NJ add 6%.). Send check or money order, no cash or C.O.D.s, please.
  To place a credit card order, call 1-800-847-8270.

NAME _____

ADDRESS _____

CITY/STATE_____ ZIP_____